Was Miranda here, then? She must be. He hadn't had time to think about it. So this was the day, then, that he…or they…had managed to put off for so long.

And there she was, right in front of him, almost exactly the way Nick remembered her—the way he'd glimpsed her two years ago, before making that very fast and very firm decision to pull back. There she was, stepping into the breach with her cheerful, elfin and slightly mischievous face, her calm, sweet voice, her practical attitude, her slim, almost tomboy build and her heart worn carelessly and innocently on her sleeve.

'Hello, Nick,' she said.

CROCODILE CREEK

**A cutting-edge medical centre.
Fully equipped for saving lives and loves!**

**Crocodile Creek's state-of-the-art
Medical Centre and Rescue Response Unit
is home to a team of expertly trained
medical professionals. These dedicated
men and women face the challenges of life,
love and medicine every day!**

**This month we meet gorgeous surgeon
Nick Devlin when he is reunited
with Miranda Carlisle**
A PROPOSAL WORTH WAITING FOR
by Lilian Darcy

**Look out for dedicated neurosurgeon
Nick Vavunis next month as he sweeps
beautiful physiotherapist Suzie off her feet**
MARRYING THE MILLIONAIRE DOCTOR
by Alison Roberts

And in the months to follow:

**Sexy Angus Stuart comes
face to face with the wife he thought he'd lost**
CHILDREN'S DOCTOR, MEANT-TO-BE WIFE
by Meredith Webber

**And December sees Crocodile Creek
Medical Director Charles Wetherby makes his
final bid to make nurse Jill his longed-for bride in**
A BRIDE AND CHILD WORTH WAITING FOR
by Marion Lennox

A PROPOSAL WORTH WAITING FOR

BY
LILIAN DARCY

MILLS & BOON®
Pure reading pleasure™

First published in Great Britain 2008
Large Print edition 2009
Harlequin Mills & Boon Limited,
Eton House, 18-24 Paradise Road,
Richmond, Surrey TW9 1SR

© Lilian Darcy 2008

ISBN: 978 0 263 20496 4

Set in Times Roman 16½ on 19 pt.
17-0309-53524

Printed and bound in Great Britain
by CPI Antony Rowe, Chippenham, Wiltshire

Bestselling romance author **Lilian Darcy** has written over seventy-five novels for Mills & Boon® Medical™ Romance, Special Edition and more. She currently lives in Australia's capital city, Canberra, with her historian husband and their four children. When she is not writing or supporting her children's varied interests, Lilian likes to quilt, garden or cook. She also loves winter sports and travel.

Lilian's career highlights include numerous appearances on romance bestseller lists, three nominations for the Romance Writers of America's prestigious RITA® Award, and translation into twenty different languages. Find out more about Lilian and her books or contact her at www.liliandarcy.com

Recent titles by the same author:

THE CHILDREN'S DOCTOR
  AND THE SINGLE MUM
LONG-LOST SON: BRAND-NEW FAMILY*
PREGNANT WITH HIS CHILD*

*Crocodile Creek

PROLOGUE

HE SAW her through the open doorway of Josh's hospital room and stopped, his body dropping instantly into a silent, wary freeze, half-masked by the door itself, while he prayed she hadn't seen him.

Miranda Carlisle.

The name shouldn't mean so much to him after so long. It had been eight years since they'd last seen each other. And if the intervening time since he and Miranda had studied medicine together provided a protective cushion, then surely his marriage to Anna should do so even more.

But my marriage is in so much trouble...

Nick shut his eyes for a moment, not willing to face the thought. He could hear Anna's murmuring voice as she sat in the chair beside Josh's bed, just out of his line of sight. She had her usual barrage of almost obsessive questions and concerns. Miranda's replies sounded patient and cheerful and clear, but he doubted whether they would quieten Anna's fears for long.

When he opened his eyes again, he saw Miranda scribbling some lines in Josh's notes, her head bent a little to reveal the delicate shape of her neck and her elfin ears showing pale pink through her silky dark hair. She still wore it in that swinging ponytail he remembered, and it made her look young and vibrantly energetic, like a jazz dancer or the leader of a troop of Guides.

She was Josh's doctor now. His new respiratory specialist, because the previous one, Dr McCubbin, had just retired. Anna was thrilled with Dr Carlisle, after Josh's emergency admission yesterday, and had said so in her usual over-detailed, stress-filled way.

But Nick hadn't admitted to their past association, other than to say to Anna in passing, 'We went through medicine together. She worked bloody hard every step of the way. I'm not surprised you think she's good.'

Good, and dangerous.

Dangerous?

He was shocked to recognise the fact, but he

was in no doubt of it. If their brief, passionate past relationship was going to flare in his memory in such vivid colours every time he saw her, then he should steer clear of her in the future as much as he could. For the sake of his very shaky marriage. For the sake of politeness and professionalism. For the sake of…yeah…a few things inside himself that it wouldn't be productive or relevant or safe at this point to confront, when there was so much else of more importance going on.

On paper, you'd think that avoiding Miranda Carlisle wouldn't be possible at all. Nick's own son. His son's doctor. The scarily unstable nature of Josh's asthma attacks. The relationship between Miranda and little Josh would definitely be ongoing.

But when Nick thought of the way Anna had been reacting to Josh's illness since it had been diagnosed eleven months ago, he knew with his usual frustration and sinking heart that his wife would be only too happy if he kept out of the way and left all the questions, the emotions and the sacrifice to her.

Now, for example. She wouldn't be pleased to

see him, wouldn't appreciate how much he'd shoved his schedule around at Royal Victoria Hospital in order to get here at this time of day.

He saw Miranda tuck Josh's notes into the plastic pocket at the end of the bed. It looked as if she was leaving. He ducked quickly back against the corridor wall before heading into the nearest visitor's toilet.

She hadn't seen him. Good. He would wait until she was certain to be gone—as a reconstructive surgeon who made these kinds of hospital rounds himself on a daily basis, he knew how to time these things—and then he'd go in to greet his wife and son.

Nick was wrong. Miranda had seen him, although she guessed he didn't know it. When he'd first appeared and then ducked back, the movement had caught her eye at once. She'd been steeling herself for the encounter, so she had been on the alert.

Her focus had been on Josh and his mother, but she'd glimpsed the figure in the doorway and managed to catch a couple more angled, hidden glances as she'd written in Josh's notes.

Handy things, those notes.

As soon as she'd seen the name Devlin, Nicholas, listed as the patient's father, she'd wondered. Her former colleague, James McCubbin, had mentioned in passing a young patient named Devlin with a surgeon for a father. Now James had retired, and his patients would be parcelled out to the other three doctors in the practice.

By virtue of being the one on call when Josh had come into the emergency department with his mother yesterday afternoon, she'd inherited him, and a quick check of the contact details had confirmed that his father was *that* Nick, *her* Nick, the one who had sneaked up on her heart without her knowing it during the course of six years of shared medical studies and had then shattered it to pieces in one single night.

Or maybe she'd broken her own heart by giving it away too eagerly. She'd never really been sure how those things went. Her fault, or his? She could see, now, how much her failed six-year relationship with Ian Mackenzie had been the result of the lessons she'd learned…or had thought she'd learned…from what had happened with Nick.

And now she was Nick's son's doctor, and he'd disappeared from the doorway, and she wondered if the reason had anything to do with her. Maybe it was only that his pager had gone off. But if he was trying to avoid her...

Well, he couldn't do that forever. At some point, they'd have to connect.

CHAPTER ONE

INCREDIBLY, it took two years.

Having taken on Josh Devlin as a patient when he was three years old, Miranda didn't see his father again until the little boy was five…

'I can't come, Miranda. I have to pull out of the whole first week. Maybe even the whole trip.' Anna Devlin looked white with stress and half-blind to anything else going on around her. She grabbed Miranda's arm in the middle of the check-in concourse at Melbourne's Tullamarine Airport and made the announcement before Miranda even had time to greet her properly.

'Hey…'

'My mother's broken her leg. She's not going to manage. It just happened today. She slipped on her front steps. I've been in six places at once, on the phone, at the hospital. And, of course, it all falls to me. My sisters are saying they can't possibly come down. I'm so sorry, Miranda. I'm a complete mess.'

'It's OK. Slow down a bit, Anna.' Miranda took a couple of controlled breaths herself in an attempt to encourage her patient's mother to find some calm. 'First, is Josh upset that you won't be going with him? Where is he?'

Anna shook her head distractedly. 'N-no, he's all right. Sort of. He's here, minding his suitcase. A bit overwhelmed. Am I doing the right thing? I can't see any other option. I'm the one who's really panicking. I'm trying not to let it show.'

Trying, and failing dismally.

Anna was often emotional and tunnel-visioned, verging on obsessive, although Miranda had tried in various ways to get her to see that it wasn't good for her son. Anna said all the right things, but couldn't put her resolutions into practice.

'Do you want to look at cancelling? Rescheduling for another time?' Over Anna's shoulder, Miranda saw two more families arrive, but there was still plenty of time. The flight to Queensland wasn't due to board for another half-hour.

Anna shook her head at Miranda's questions. 'No, Josh would be so disappointed. We've been talking about it for weeks. No, he definitely has to go. It would take months to schedule him another stay, wouldn't it?'

'Probably,' Miranda had to admit.

Places at the Crocodile Creek Kids' Camp on Wallaby Island off the coast of northern Queensland were in high demand. Miranda had a zing in her spirits this afternoon, herself, even though she was going there not on a private holiday but in her professional capacity.

Anna let go of her arm at last and she spotted five-year-old Josh just a few metres away, sitting obediently on his suitcase near the check-in counter. He looked far more calm than his mother. Too calm, maybe. A little subdued. He was still essentially the same kid Miranda had first met two years ago—small for his age, endearingly gap-toothed and urchin-like, a real sweetheart with a healthy capacity for mischief and numerous hospital admissions under his belt. Anna was totally and single-mindedly devoted to him, and he was her only child.

There wouldn't be any more now.

Anna and Nick were divorced.

'He'll be fine,' she promised Anna. 'We'll take care of him. We have a couple of other kids coming without parents.'

She gestured towards awkward, unconfident Stella Vavunis, aged thirteen, whom she'd already ticked off on her list. Stella's dad was supposed to be coming later in the week. As one of the major donors to the new medical centre on Wallaby Island, he would be a guest of honour at Saturday's official opening. For the first few days, however, Stella would be on her own.

In remission from bone cancer, Stella wasn't one of Miranda's own patients, but her heart went out to the girl anyway. Her dark hair was growing back wispy and thin after her chemo, and she'd lost the lower half of her right leg. Adept on her elbow crutches, she was intensely self-conscious about her lost limb and had her new prosthesis covered in a pair of heavy jeans that would be way too hot for the climate of North Queensland.

'He's not coming without a parent,' Anna announced, her stress level visibly rising again.

She had an exotic, compelling kind of beauty, with huge eyes, high cheekbones and full lips, and the combination of her good looks and high emotion had begun to draw some attention.

Miranda frowned, a little slow. *Too* slow, considering how long she'd been waiting for something like this to happen. 'But...?'

'That's the whole thing, Miranda.' Miranda's arm was once again captured in a tight grip. 'That's the whole reason—well, a big part of it—why I'm so stressed.' She added in a tone that was half wail, half whisper, 'He's coming with Nick.'

Right. With Nick.

She must have looked shocked—and shouldn't have let it show—because Anna said in a tight voice, 'Please. Don't make me dread this any more than I am already. Don't make Josh dread it, especially.'

'I didn't mean—'

'Nick should be here within the next ten minutes. He promised me he wouldn't muck me around on this.'

'So he's coming for the whole two weeks? At such short notice?'

Anna rolled her eyes and drawled, 'I know. It's a miracle. Actually making a sacrifice for his son for once.'

'Well, I meant—' Miranda meant that it was a miracle, just as Anna had said, but without the other woman's edge of sarcasm and bitterness. It was great that the persistently absent surgeon could step in to fill the breach, just hours in advance of the flight. Her initial shocked gut reaction was her own problem, not Anna's.

'I'm hoping it'll only be for the first week,' Anna was saying. 'I'm going to find a way to get up there for the second week if it kills me! Two weeks with Nick will ruin Josh's stay.'

Had the little boy heard? Miranda wondered. Anna wasn't sufficiently careful in what she said around her son.

Whether it was one week or two, Nick must have called in some favours, Miranda realised. He would have made a lot of phone calls that morning to get everything organised and taken care of. His willingness to make the effort did surprise her somewhat, when she thought about it. She'd been forced, by his persistent non-appearance, to the conclusion that he was a very uninvolved parent, and the fact bothered her more than it should.

Anna and Nick had been divorced for months, now, but even before that, Anna was always the parent who brought Josh in for appointments, always the one who phoned with questions, and whose signature appeared on admission and consent forms when Josh was in hospital.

Miranda knew that Nick had made the odd appearance since that first time when she'd seen him pause and stand half-hidden by the open door. She'd seen his name in Josh's patient notes a couple of times—'7 p.m. Dad visited.' But they'd never come face to face. To be honest, for reasons that she didn't want to examine too closely, she'd been relieved about that. Maybe she'd even contributed to it, in how she timed her hospital visits and routine check-ups.

Their failure to connect with each other gave a nagging, unfinished quality to her memories of their past, however. Everything she knew about Nick Devlin's attitudes and behaviour as a father over the past couple of years she'd heard from Anna. Very little of it was good. Nick was

apparently cool, distant and uncaring, and Josh
shrank from him whenever father and son were
together.

Funny how things happened.

Years ago, younger and more naive about men
in general and about Nick Devlin in particular,
Miranda would have predicted he'd make a great
father. She was so sure that in their one night
together she had suddenly seen—had been
allowed to see—beyond the arrogant, unap-
proachable exterior to the person he really was.
But apparently she hadn't understood him
anywhere near as accurately and deeply as she'd
thought back then.

Ships that passed in the night, and all that.
Women were sometimes way too good at
kidding themselves about that stuff. Was that the
problem? Her own poor judgement? Had she
learned enough since then to avoid similar
mistakes in future? The memories were still
strong, but Miranda didn't trust them any more.
She *must* have read him wrong when they'd
been medical students together. A wife—even
an ex-wife—would know him better.

How am I going to feel about seeing him?
For better or for worse, she was about to find out.

Nick paid off the cab driver, grabbed his duffel bag from beside the kerb and headed for the terminal. He'd promised Anna that he wouldn't be late and he wasn't.

Or almost wasn't.

He'd had a sick-making fifteen minutes of panic at home about what he should be bringing for his son, and as usual he couldn't deal with the strength of the emotion because it brought so much other stuff with it.

He had some snacks and a drink for the flight, a couple of picture books and the kind of cheap toy that a five-year-old kid could play with on an aircraft tray table, and Anna would have Josh's asthma gear, of course, as well as his clothing, but...

Should he be bringing a proper gift? A camera, or snorkelling equipment? He already had Josh's Christmas present, a substantial addition to his Lego collection. Should he bring that, make it a going-away treat, and get him something else for Christmas, which was still two months away? Or did that smack far too much of an attempt to bribe his son for love?

The decision paralysed him.

Yes, he, Dr Nicholas Devlin, MB BS FRACS, Plastic and Reconstructive Surgeon at Melbourne's renowned Royal Victoria Hospital, who was normally able to make life-altering decisions in seconds if he had to, could not for the life of him decide how to handle the issue of his son's gift.

He knew what Anna would say. 'Oh, no, Nick, you didn't!'

Inevitably, whatever decision he made, it would be drastically and utterly the wrong one as far as she was concerned. It was a pathological condition in their impossible relationship, and a basic tenet of her maternal faith, that everything he did with, or to, or for their asthma-stricken son, everything he felt, everything he planned and almost every word he said, was and always had been wrong.

Although this was probably not the major reason for their divorce, it hadn't helped, and things hadn't improved since.

OK, so since he couldn't win no matter what he did, he'd go with his own convictions and not try to second-guess what she would want. Unless she asked directly, he wouldn't tell her about what he had and hadn't brought for Josh. The Lego could stay at home, and if Josh wanted to take photos or try snorkelling, they'd pick up what they needed on the spot.

Decision made.

Jaw squared.

Emotion pushed safely below the surface where it couldn't get in the way.

Sorted.

By the time he'd thrown off the panic and the bitterness, remembered how to act like a surgeon instead of a powerless and frustrated non-custodial parent, and realised he hadn't yet called for a taxi, a vital fifteen minutes had passed and he was running late.

He saw Anna's pale, accusing face as he approached the check-in concourse. She must have been looking for him, scanning for his figure above the heads of the crowd.

And she *wanted* him to be late. He knew it. Later than this. Really, unforgivably, flagrantly, uncaringly late, so that she could tell people about it—'Can you *believe* he missed the flight?

Josh had to go up *on his own*!'—and it would count as yet another black mark against his name.

'What happened?' she asked with angry accusation as soon as he came up to her, as if she expected at minimum a six-car pile-up on the freeway.

'Taxi.' He'd stopped making lengthy excuses long ago. Had stopped arguing, stopped appealing to her common sense and her notion of justice, stopped trying to get her to see how obsessively over-protective she was, and how much she shut him out of their son's life. Maybe she was right to consider that he didn't belong there, he sometimes felt.

Before he could get past her to greet Josh, Anna delivered a stinging, rapid-fire round of instructions about their son's care and finished, 'Nick, if you stuff this up, Josh has a miserable time, I will *kill* you!'

Ignoring the threat to his life, which his ex-wife found a reason to hit him with almost every time they spoke, he said through a tight jaw, 'I'm not going to stuff this up. Why do you think I would?'

'Because you never take his health seriously

enough. Because you hardly know him, and he hardly knows you. He doesn't trust you.'

'And that's my fault, is it?' he added quickly, almost growling the words, 'Forget it, forget it.' They'd been through that one a thousand times. 'Look, I know you're not happy about this. But Josh and I will be fine.' He took a deep breath and prepared himself to say the L-word. 'I love my son, Anna, and don't you ever, ever dare to suggest otherwise!'

'Love isn't enough,' she muttered, turning away from him so that her face was screened by her well-cut fall of light brown hair. 'Nowhere near enough.'

For her, it was a pretty generous concession, so he left the subject alone, said a stilted goodbye, and looked over at Josh, his stomach already sinking at the thought of what he might see in his son's face.

Indifference. Dislike. Fear…

Anna reached their little boy first, of course. While Nick was still three paces away, she bent down and engulfed Josh in a huge, constricting hug as she prepared to say goodbye. She was actually shaking, Nick saw, as she let forth an intense stream of words close to his ear. Nick only caught a few words. 'Don't want…terrified…every single minute.'

Josh nodded. Was he wheezing? What the hell was Anna saying? That she was terrified?

'And you'll phone if there are any problems,' she finished, beginning to stand so that Nick could hear her better. 'Anything that's making you unhappy.'

If Dad is making you unhappy, Nick heard in her tone. At least she managed not to say it out loud for once. He stepped forward. 'Go, Anna,' he said, more calmly than he felt. 'Josh and I will be fine, won't we, little guy?'

'Don't call him that,' Anna snarled through the side of her mouth, and tore herself away, disappearing behind a noisy tour group before he could reply.

Hell.

He'd meant it as an endearment. If Josh was sensitive about being small for his age, Nick hadn't known. But, then, how would he? Anna made it so difficult for them to spend any real time together, and she never willingly shared her insights about their son. If Josh was wary and distant, it was her doing, wasn't it?

Or was it his own lack of perception that was the problem? His tendency to pull back when emotions grew risky and ran high? His reluctance to show his deepest feelings?

A wave of self-doubt washed over him and he stepped away, didn't drop into a Josh-level squat as he'd intended and wanted to, didn't pick up the colourful backpack with the inhalers and spacer and written asthma action plan inside, even though he could definitely hear that Josh was wheezing. And he didn't put his arm around his son's little shoulder in case Josh pushed him away.

This kind of self-doubt had been such a rare thing in his life until Josh's birth that he still didn't know how to handle it. He'd been taught to believe in himself, to act as if he was in the right even when he wasn't, to keep the façade of strength and ego and self-control in place at all times, no matter what he might be feeling inside. He'd doubted himself at times, of course, but he'd always mastered it, never let it hold him back.

The slow, horrible breakdown of his marriage to Anna and the gulf in their attitudes to Josh had thrown a new light on everything he'd thought he knew about himself, and it was still doing so. Did he listen to the doubts, ignore them, or shoot them down?

In a stark moment of anguish, he decided that Anna was right. He and Josh didn't know each other or trust each other well enough to be doing this—going away together, going to camp, father and son. He blamed her for it, but however it had happened…perhaps he was more at fault than he'd ever admitted…it was a reality. He felt ill-equipped and at sea, daunted at the prospect of fulfilling all Anna's dire predictions and fears, and messing this up.

Hurting Josh.

Scaring him off.

Saying and doing all the wrong things.

Sabotaging the holiday's hopes and promises the way he'd sabotaged his personal life in so many other ways.

'Dr Carlisle?' Josh's voice sounded small and scared.

Dr Carlisle…

'Dr Carlisle, I think I need to use my inhaler.'

The name jolted Nick out of his negative thoughts. Was Miranda here, then? Was she— hell!—*coming* on this camp? She must be. Of course there would be medical people accompanying the group. He hadn't had time to think about it. So this was the day, then, that he…or they…had managed to put off for so long.

'Hey, are you wheezing?'

And there she was, right in front of him, almost exactly the way Nick remembered her, the way he'd glimpsed her two years ago, before making that very fast and very firm decision to pull back. There she was, stepping into the breach with her cheerful, elfin and slightly mischievous face, her calm, sweet voice, her practical attitude, her slim, almost boyish build and her heart worn carelessly and innocently on her sleeve.

'Hello, Nick,' she said.

Ten years. Miranda wasn't going to count the near-miss from two years ago. Of course he remembered her and knew exactly who she was, exactly where she fitted into his past. She saw it in his face, when he reached out a hand for her to shake. 'We haven't…uh…managed to connect since you started treating Josh,' he said.

He wore the same aura of cool and rather distant confidence that she recognised, and that she'd only once seen truly and seriously slip. He used his body the same way, too. He never paraded his height or the strength in his shoulders, but, then, a man didn't need to when he was as tall and strong as Nick. He was imposing without even trying.

'No, we haven't.'

On the surface, their words took care of the subject, but she strongly suspected it would come up again.

Physically, he'd barely changed. His lightly tanned skin had done a little more living, and it showed in the fine creases beginning to form around his eyes and mouth. His body had hardened. She could imagine him running several kilometres a day, or going for gym sessions at six in the morning before starting surgery or hospital rounds.

'Anna has a lot of confidence in you,' he added, 'which is great.'

'I'm glad you were able to come at such short notice,' she told him. And meant it, because ten years was a long time, and this man was a patient's father now, nothing more. She had to remember that. *Had* to. Hell, what was the alternative? 'It'll be great for Josh to have his dad there.'

'You think?'

'Well, yes.'

Didn't he agree? Was that a cynical drawl, or something else? Anna had been very nervous and wound up about the whole thing, which was typical, but her fears did have some basis in reality—at least as far as Josh's health was concerned. Maybe the man seriously didn't want to be in for this assignment, and his reluctance and lack of interest would ruin Josh's whole camp experience.

But Miranda couldn't think about that abstract possibility right now. In fact, she couldn't think about Nick Devlin at all. She had to deal with the concrete reality that Josh's asthma attack was getting more severe by the second. With a sinking heart, she saw the Allandales arriving with their thirteen-year-old daughter—verging on late, heavily laden with luggage, instantly wanting and expecting her full attention, as they always did.

Pretending she hadn't seen them, she bent down to take Josh's backpack, wanting to pull out his inhaler and spacer. His breathing was getting worse and he looked increasingly distressed as the seconds passed. He was scrabbling at his backpack now, trying to get it open, but the zip seemed to be stuck and he hadn't considered his father as a possible source of help.

'Give the backpack to me, sweetheart,' Miranda urged him. 'Don't try to do it yourself. You just keep breathing, OK?'

'Dr Carlisle!' Rick Allandale reached her, his knees roughly at her eye level.

Cutting off what would probably be a lengthy list of questions, explanations or complaints, none of which she needed now, she told him, 'Let me tick Lauren's name off on my list in a minute, Mr Allandale. We're waiting until everyone's here before we check in.'

'Do you know his action plan off the top of your head?' Nick asked in her ear.

Miranda felt rather than saw him. He'd squatted down to Josh's level, just as she had done, and his well-muscled upper arm bumped her shoulder while his backside rested on his heels. She caught the faint waft of some very pleasant male grooming product. Aftershave or shampoo, or maybe just plain old soap.

He didn't wait for her answer. 'Because I do. You have other people to take care of. Let me handle this.'

'Everyone else can wait,' she answered, not sure if he understood the urgency. He must surely realise that the attack was being exacerbated by Josh's mix of anxiety and over-excitement.

Too aware that he hadn't moved further away, Miranda uncapped the Ventolin inhaler and attached it to the spacer, helped Josh get the other end of the spacer ready at his lips. 'OK, ready to breathe out? Now...'

But Josh couldn't concentrate and, even with the spacer, he mistimed the dose and took the spacer from his lips too soon. Miranda saw a puff like smoke as most of the drug escaped into the air.

Lauren Allandale was watching Josh's struggle for breath and his clumsiness with the inhaler, as were a couple of other kids and a parent or two. The atmosphere was chaotic and claustrophobic. Another big group of tourists had just arrived, ready to check in for their flight, and the tour leader was yelling instructions to them in a language Miranda couldn't identify. Korean? More stares arrowed in Josh's direction.

'Please, let me deal with this,' Nick repeated, needing to lean close to keep a shred of privacy for his son. Miranda felt the warmth of his body, let herself meet his brown gaze for a moment and found it far too familiar. He wasn't smiling. His expression was motionless, almost forbidding, and yet it stirred her and filled her with memories. Suddenly, as she'd feared all along, ten years wasn't very much time at all. 'You have other things to attend to. And he's my son.'

'You're confident that you know what to do?' She felt their fingers touch briefly as he took the inhaler and spacer out of her hands. Should she grab the equipment back?

'For heck's sake, I'm a doctor!'

'I mean, the exact dosage. The frequency.'

'Yes, I do,' he told her shortly, shoving the equipment into Josh's backpack. 'The very first thing I'm going to do is take him somewhere quiet. We can't get him focused and relaxed here. I saw signs for a parents' room.' He spoke to his son, turning a shoulder to shut Miranda out, whether through hostility or because she just wasn't important at the moment she didn't know. 'Josh, come with me and we'll get you breathing again, shall we?' His voice sounded stiff and almost formal. 'We don't want you having to go to bed as soon as we get there. We want to get out exploring, right?'

Josh nodded, but his eyes were still wide with effort and fear. Fear of not being able to breathe? Or of something else?

'When's the latest we can get back here for check-in?' Nick asked Miranda. 'Twelve-forty? Don't hold the group up, will you?'

'Your baggage…' she recalled. You couldn't check in someone else's bags, neither did Security take an innocent view of luggage left unattended.

'I'll wait with it,' said Benita Green, the nurse who had come with the cancer kids' group.

Miranda and Nick both nodded at the same time. 'Thanks.'

Then Nick scooped up Josh and carried him off, the little backpack with its bright colours and cartoon motif swinging incongruously from one big male shoulder as he strode at a rapid pace through the terminal. Josh looked so light and small and vulnerable in his arms, his little body stiff and his shoulders lifting with his effort to breathe.

* * *

Nick found the parents' room with no difficulty.

It was like most such places, a small, bland room whose main virtue was its quietness and lack of crowds. Josh's breathing had continued to worsen as Nick carried him and he had to fight his own sense of growing panic.

What if he couldn't get an effective dose? What if Josh's habitual wariness around him made him unable to relax enough to throw off the attack? What medical equipment did the airport medical centre have? It was close by. They'd just passed it. Should Nick have gone directly there instead of attempting to deal with this attack on his own?

Was he in some kind of denial, as Anna had so often accused? Or was this trip to the parents' room a piece of misplaced heroism on his part? Anna had accused him of that in the past, too. What if this whole precious, scary, miraculously out-of-the-blue week or more with his son was derailed at the very start by another hospital stay?

I want this. I want time with my son.

Even though it challenged his self-confidence on almost every level.

I want the two of us to defeat this asthma monster together, in the next ten minutes, to prove to both of us that we can. I want him to love me, and to know that I love him.

'OK, this is better, isn't it?' he said to Josh. 'Nobody watching.'

He dropped the backpack from his shoulder, grabbed the inhaler and spacer from where he'd flung them inside. 'Now, show me how you do this. Show me your very best breath out and then a huge breath in, after you press.'

Josh pressed the inhaler, breathed in and out while Nick counted the breaths and kept a gentle grip on the spacer. His son still hadn't spoken a word.

'Good. That was great,' he said, pushing encouragement into his voice. 'Is that feeling any better?'

Josh nodded but still didn't speak. Nick thought he detected a mild improvement but second-guessed the impression at once, as usual. Maybe it was only that the panicky look had softened a bit in a quieter atmosphere.

He had a powerful, gut-dropping need for Miranda to be there, remembering six years of her common sense and sweetness and warmth and diligence and brains, during lectures and tutorial groups and anatomy lab sessions, followed by that one intense night of her body in bed and hours and hours of talking. Remembering it all as if it were yesterday that they'd finished medicine together. Just those few minutes of talking with her near the check-in desk had brought it all back, as he'd somehow known for the past two years that it would.

But she wasn't there, so he and Josh just had to wait, find some patience and some trust on their own.

And administer a second dose of Ventolin, Nick decided, as the first one wasn't working the miracle cure he'd hoped for. Time was getting on, but if he pushed Josh to go back to the check-in desk too soon…

So how did they pass the time until the next dose? There were no toys in here, no windows, nothing. Just him and Josh, on their own together for the first time in how long…probably three months…waiting to see if he could breathe.

'How about a story?' Nick suggested, and heard his voice come out too hearty.

With a wheezy effort, not looking at him, Josh answered, 'We have to…go back and…meet the others…and get on the…plane.'

His heart sinking, Nick checked his watch so he'd know when to give the next dose. 'Not yet, little guy,' he said, then mentally cursed himself for repeating the phrase Anna had frowned at.

It was a term of endearment, damn it!

Find another one, he decided. Whether she's right or wrong, play it safe, take the line of least resistance, for Josh's sake. And for his own?

It was what he'd been doing for far too long.

CHAPTER TWO

'THEY'LL be closing the flight in twenty minutes, Miranda,' Benita said. 'What do you think has happened to Josh and his dad? They wouldn't have just wandered into a shop to buy post-cards?'

'I'm getting worried,' Miranda admitted. Nick and his son had been absent for fifteen minutes—enough time to administer the first dose of Ventolin and assess its effect. If it wasn't working…

It often didn't. Despite long-term treatment to develop Josh's lungs, on top of a regimen of preventative action which Anna stuck to like a monk's ritual, Josh's sudden attacks had pro-gressed three times in the past year to the point where hospital admission had been the only option.

If that happened now…

She felt a surge of disappointment on Josh's

behalf. He'd been looking forward to this trip so much. Possibly *too* much. Miranda had privately wondered if any place in the whole world could match the paradise of Crocodile Creek Kids' Camp and Wallaby Island as they existed in little Josh's energetic imagination.

He'd said to her at his last check-up, 'There'll be waterfalls and birds and lakes *teeming* with crocodiles, and rides and surf and the best food, and toys and campfires and sing-alongs, and I'm going to swim all day, except when I'm feeding the crocodiles. I'm not going in the water with *them*! They're in a lake, they're not in the ocean or the pool. And I think the lake is going to be purple. And fireworks. There has to be fireworks.'

And Miranda had smiled at him and nodded, 'Purple, huh?' And, of course, it was good that he was looking forward to it so much, but kids could make themselves sick with excitement, and then Nick had had to come on the holiday instead of Anna, which added a level of stress and uncertainty to the excitement, and—

'I'm going to go and hunt them up,' Miranda told Benita. 'Can you handle things here, and guard Nick and Josh's luggage? If I can't get them to the check-in in the next twenty-five minutes at the outside, bad luck. We can't have the whole group miss the flight because of two people.'

Even if one of them was one of her favourite patients, and the other one was…

Well, was Nick Devlin.

A very memorable ship passing in the night, practically scraping her all down the starboard side like the *Titanic* and its famous iceberg, and pushing her off course for far too long.

She hurried through the terminal, found the parents' room and knocked on the door. 'Nick? Josh? Are you still in there?'

Nick opened the door. He looked anxious, jittery and too light on his feet. He wanted action and control and to get on that plane *now*. Miranda was shocked at the way she could read his emotional state. No, not just read it, feel it as if it was happening inside her own body. As soon as he saw her, he gave a frowning glance at his watch and she knew what he must be thinking.

Can we do this?

Behind him Josh sat on a bland vinyl chair. Still wheezing. Not noticeably better, but not worse. *Could* they do this, with time squeezing them as tight as Josh's lungs?

Miranda felt steely determination set in.

Could they? Just try showing her any other option!

'Time for a second dose,' she said. 'Let's not have you two miss the flight. There isn't another connecting hop out to the island until tomorrow afternoon.'

'We've just done a second lot,' Nick muttered, blocking the conversation from Josh's ears with the bulk of his body in the half-open doorway. His open-necked shirt showed a fine mist of perspiration across his collar-bone. He was literally sweating this—the tight timing, Josh's breathing, the potential disappointment. 'What do you think? Is there any point hanging on here for a third, or should I give up now and cancel our flight? Give up on the whole thing?'

She couldn't keep back a stricken sound. Cancel Josh's trip?

'I'm asking you as a doctor, Miranda,' he added, as if he knew that she was operating far too much on emotion right now. 'Not as someone who wants my little boy to have his holiday. Should we really push this? Is it a sign that I'm not the right person to be…? No, hell, I can't think straight about any of this. You need to be the one to make the decision.'

He met her gaze, jaw tight, expression rigid, fighting himself. She wasn't imagining the appeal reflecting from deep within his brown eyes. It was there, even though he'd never been the kind of man to show any weakness easily or willingly.

Somehow, his look cut to the heart of her just as the whole of him had cut to the heart of her ten years ago, during their one night together, without him apparently even knowing it. Or if he had known, back then, he hadn't cared.

At some level he trusted her on this, she decided—trusted Anna's assessment of her as a professional, or his own more personal memories. The fact warmed her too much and she had to push the feeling away. She should remember that after their night of talking and making love, which she'd believed in so much, he'd never phoned…

'Has he improved at all?' she asked quickly.

'A little. More after the dose I gave him a couple of minutes ago. I—I don't think he trusts me. Is he psyching himself out because I'm here, not his mother? Maybe at some level this is happening because he doesn't want to go to camp with me.'

He was being incredibly careful not to let Josh hear. Miranda had to step closer and keep her eyes fixed on that barely moving mouth but still she strained to hear him. At this distance, she could see more clearly the lines on his face that hadn't been there ten years ago, and she had a totally unacceptable urge to soothe them with her fingers.

'Let's not think that way. Let me take a look at him,' she suggested.

'He knows you almost better than he knows me, I guess.' The words, barely more than a mutter, cut Miranda to the heart.

She came fully into the parents' room and dropped to Josh-level. He was sitting in the room's one chair. 'Can you talk, Josh?'

'A bit.'

'You said the second dose helped?' She could feel Nick behind her, a ball of strong and very male tension and distress. He really didn't want to cancel this trip.

'Yes.'

'So we'll just sit here, shall we, and then we'll give a third dose and that'll do the trick.' She spoke as if there was no other possibility, and Josh smiled at last.

While Nick let out a sigh that she didn't dare to think came from relief.

Not yet, Nick, please.

Josh wasn't out of the woods yet.

Ten minutes later, they both helped him with the third dose, then Nick put his asthma equipment back in the colouful backpack and they listened to the wonderful sound of Josh breathing better and talking again. 'Did we miss the plane?'

'No, sweetheart. We have time.'

Not much of it, though.

Nick took her aside again, holding her arm, bending his head towards hers so that the dark hair spilling across his forehead almost brushed her face. 'Can we really do this? What if he crashes again during the flight?' His touch felt impossibly familiar, even after so long. She couldn't believe how quickly they'd reconnected in such a personal way.

Maybe because she'd been expecting something like this—half dreading and half wanting it—for two years? It was harder than if he'd simply shown up in her life again, out of the blue.

'They have oxygen on board,' Miranda answered, 'and the fact that he's responded to these first few doses is a good sign. In the past, when he's crashed badly, it's been downhill all the way.'

'True,' Nick said. 'Ambulance ride to the hospital. The full works.'

'He's been very excited about this trip.'

'Don't I know it!'

'I so-o-o don't want to pull the plug on it for him now.'

'Neither do I,' Nick said.

'Is it the excitement, do you think?' Miranda asked him quietly.

'That and…' He stopped, took a breath and readied himself to choose his words carefully. 'Anna can't…uh…always hide when she's stressed. He picks up on it far too much. As far as she's concerned, the timing of her mother's accident couldn't have been worse, and maybe she's right…'

Anna's emotions sometimes made Josh sicker. Nick and Miranda were in agreement on that.

But then he added, 'And maybe she's right to think it'll be disastrous to have me with him on the trip. He and I haven't spent as much time together as I'd like.'

He hated saying those outwardly bland words, Miranda could tell. Hated saying them because they were true? Or because they weren't? Had he genuinely *wanted* a better relationship with his son all along? Or was Anna right in saying, as she frequently did, that Nick was the one to withdraw?

His smile was forced. 'We looked at pictures of a Very Greedy Frog.'

'As much time as you'd like with him?' she echoed, before she could stop herself. It had sounded a little too much like a challenge— *Yeah, really? That's not what Anna says.* Why had she felt the need to plumb the level of his honesty now, when they were in such a rush?

He looked at her and she could almost see him mentally prioritising his battles. Most important, get himself and Josh onto the flight. Way down the list, argue with his son's respiratory physician about which divorced parent most deserved the prize for honesty and clear thinking and sacrifice.

'Look, is there still time?' he asked. 'That's what's important now.'

'You're right. I'm sorry. Benita has been waiting with your luggage. Everyone else will have gone through by now. We have to get to that check-in desk *now*, if you're going to make the flight.'

He nodded for the third time. Wasn't going to waste words when he didn't have that luxury. Once again, he scooped Josh into his arms and slung the backpack over one shoulder. 'Let's do it. Josh, can you breathe?'

No answer.

'Josh, can you? You have to talk to me!'

'Yes. I'm breathing.'

'I'll put you down later, so you can walk onto the plane on your own, OK? For now I'm carrying you, because we need to hurry.'

'So are we still going?' came a thin little voice.

'Well, do you want to?' Wooden tone.

'Yes!'

'With me?'

'Y-yes.' A lot less emphatic.

'Good,' Nick said, and suddenly hugged him fiercely. 'Because I think we're going to have a great time.' His voice was thick with sudden emotion that almost brought tears to Miranda's eyes.

He cared. Whatever else she might doubt about him now, she couldn't doubt that.

They almost ran through the terminal.

A sympathetic desk clerk, who'd been told about the situation, waved them through to the first-class check-in desk and despatched their luggage along the conveyor with practised speed. Waiting in a queue to go through Security, they heard the announcement for final boarding for the flight, but Nick said stoically, 'They've let our baggage through, and the desk clerk knows we're on our way. They should hold the flight a few minutes for us, now. I hope,' he added.

Their departure gate seemed miles away, at the far end of the concourse. Nick loped ahead, seeming untroubled by Josh's light weight. Miranda struggled to keep up. Last night's sleepless mental list-checking of today's travel details was taking its toll. Finally she saw the gate lounge and the open door leading to the access tunnel. The area was bare of passengers and a member of the ground crew was speaking into a telephone.

'Boarding pass?' Nick barked at Miranda.

'Right here. You've got yours and Josh's?'

'Yes.' To the ground crew he said, 'Nick Devlin, Josh Devlin, Miranda Carlisle.'

'Good. You're the three we've been waiting for.'

Breathless, Miranda followed Nick down the tunnel, the blood beating in her ears and her limbs weak with relief. They'd made it. Just. Josh was smiling. Everything was going to be OK.

Just inside the plane, they caught up with the final members of the Crocodile Creek group. Benita mimed fanning herself with relief and said, 'I'd almost given up on you.'

'So had I. But I couldn't let them miss the flight.' Miranda lowered her voice. 'Not these two. Not little Josh.'

'Be careful of that,' Benita warned. She meant the favouritism.

'I know.'

Miranda saw the Allandales blocking the aisle further down as they sorted through their cabin luggage. Stella Vavunis stood just ahead, handing over her crutches to an attendant, to be stowed in one of their special hidey-holes for the duration of the flight because they were too long for the overhead carrier bins.

The teenager's head hung with embarrassment, and her body was stiff and hunched, as if she just wanted to disappear. She felt humiliated and angry at the whole world about being singled out this way, and having to hop and hobble to her seat. Miranda thought she heard some very rude words muttered under Stella's breath.

'She isn't handling that prosthesis very well yet, is she?' Miranda murmured to Benita. 'It says in her notes it was fitted a week ago.'

'She won't even try, according to her physio,' the nurse answered. 'She hates it, still insists on using the crutches because then she can get away with looking as if she has a broken leg.'

'There's a physiotherapist visiting the camp every day. I've had a couple of phone conversations with her. Susie Jackson. She sounds nice.'

'We're all nice, Miranda!' Benita said.

'True. You're saying nice isn't enough, in a case like this.'

Nice. The word dovetailed with some of Miranda's questions about Nick, too, and about why she hadn't yet been able to give her heart to a man who truly wanted it. Was being *nice* the problem? Too nice. Nothing but nice. *Nice* wasn't enough, and sometimes it was boring…

'Stella has to be motivated,' Benita was saying. 'She has to believe what we tell her, she has to find someone she'll really listen to and trust. The prosthesis is too much reality for her right now. The crutches are what she knows, and she's sticking to them.'

'Tough for a thirteen-year-old, when body-image issues are so huge at that age already.'

'I know, but she's so darned prickly and negative and ungrateful I want to shake her, sometimes.' Benita gave a rueful shrug. 'We rub each other up the wrong way, I'm afraid, she and I. I'm not as patient as I should be.'

'That's a pity.'

'I shouldn't admit to it, should I, but you know how it is,' Benita said. 'Some you love, some you don't, often without even knowing why.'

'True,' Miranda replied, watching Nick and Josh.

Benita was right. Again. When it came to love, you often didn't know why.

'I have to fight to hide it, to be honest,' she was

saying. 'Her dad's supposed to be coming later in the week.'

'Yes, that's in our notes. He's a major donor to the rebuilt camp and medical centre.'

'And very driven. As well as very rich! I won't be surprised if something gets in the way of him making it. I don't think Stella will be surprised either, and I really, really wish I could step in and fill the breach, but we just don't get on, she and I. I get more glares from her than words. Hope she finds a friend or two this week. Someone she can talk to.'

'Someone better than just the usual *nice*, you mean?'

Benita smiled ruefully. 'That's right.'

The passengers blocking the aisles took their seats one by one, and Miranda found her own group of patients towards the back of the plane. There were three empty seats left, all in a row. Just ahead of her, Josh was walking on his own, as his dad had promised, with Nick directly behind him.

'There's your seat, mate,' he said to his son, the 'mate' part sounding a little forced and unnatural. 'Right by the window.' Josh climbed eagerly towards it, sneakers treading squarely in the middle of the two seats adjacent. 'Oh, hell, Josh, don't tread on the seat with those shoes!'

Too late. The deed was done.

Josh looked scared when he understood the reason for his dad's disapproval, even though Nick was telegraphing only a second or two of mild anger. The little boy's sneaker soles looked clean...sort of...but they had that deeply grooved tread that harboured every piece of grit and every grass clipping until just the wrong moment.

'Hope your neighbour isn't wearing a white silk dress,' Miranda said to him, smiling. She wanted to diffuse the difficult moment between father and son. Nick could see the expression on his son's face and didn't like it, she could tell.

But Nick didn't smile at her teasing comment. Once again, was she being too nice? 'Actually, it looks to me as if my neighbour is going to be you.'

'Lucky for you, then,' she persisted. 'I don't even own a white silk dress.'

Why had she bothered? Once again, he didn't smile back. She sat down beside him and felt his tightly coiled body like a piece of humming machinery just inches away.

Miranda was in demand for most of the flight.

The aisle seat was either a deliberate choice on her part or a lucky bonus, because she had to hop up and down every five minutes to answer the summons of a hand waved over someone's head and the call of her name.

Somebody needed their in-flight snack to be delivered early. Someone else had forgotten to pack painkillers and had a headache. Did Miranda happen to have some on her?

She dealt with it all cheerfully, and Nick was torn between regret that they didn't get the smallest opportunity for a proper conversation and relief because he didn't know what on earth they would find to say, with so much past and so much distance in between.

They'd studied medicine in the same pro-gramme and graduated as doctors at the same time. He'd been incredibly focused on his studies back then, knowing that nothing less than a cream-of-the-crop performance would satisfy his father.

And his father was right about so many things.

You did have to work hard to get where you wanted to go in life. You did have to keep a clear head and a strong focus and not step back to let others through first. With a whole lot of life's biggest challenges, you only got one chance. Mess things up, and that chance was gone forever. Blow off your work with drugs or alcohol, fast cars, garage rock bands or loose women, and you could so easily fail.

Some of his father's tenets of faith Nick was no longer so sure about, but those ones he still basically believed.

So he'd worked and he'd focused, hadn't married or fallen seriously in love or gone out with endless strings of girls during his university years the way some people had. He'd kept his distance from Miranda the way he'd kept his distance from almost everyone. His fellow medical students hadn't been friends but future professional rivals. But he'd noticed her, during the classes they'd taken together—noticed her more than either of them had realised at the time—and she'd told him that the same was true for her.

He'd admired the way she managed to win the

approval of various crusty or supercilious pro-
fessors without playing teacher's pet. He'd heard
the clever, perceptive, diligently researched
answers she gave to knotty medical problems
posed in class or during their earnest stints of
hospital observation. He'd seen the way she
worked and focused, just the way he did. He'd
liked the way she smiled and the way she
danced, the few times they'd gone out in the
same group.

She'd liked his laugh, and the way he would
say something funny sometimes when nobody
was expecting it. She'd liked the way his questions always pinpointed exactly the areas that
other students were unsure about. She'd liked the
fact that he never featured in lurid, gossipy
stories of drunkenness or womanising.

And then, one critical night ten years ago, after
they'd already known each other for six years,
casually, as fellow students, he'd let his guard
down and they'd spent fourteen uninterrupted
hours together at someone's party and beyond—
couldn't remember the guy's name any more—
and had fallen for each other the way the moon
had fallen into orbit around the earth.

Thinking about it, he discovered that it still scared him.

The suddenness of it. The strength. The things he'd told her. The vulnerability he'd shown. The power he'd given her over his emotions, just in one short night. It was as if a lifetime of well-schooled stoicism had broken down all at once. When a dam broke, it didn't simply spring a leak, it flooded. Everything pent up inside him had broken that night, because of her, and had come flooding out.

With her. To her. For her.

'I love you, Miranda.'

Unstoppable. Crystal clear. Terrifying.

They'd been drinking, of course, but not that much. He hadn't been hungover the next day. At the point when he'd really begun talking to her, he had downed maybe three beers in three hours. The words had exhilarated him as he spoke them, like jumping out of a plane with a parachute on his back—terror and freedom mixed like a potent cocktail, making him dizzy and wild. How many times had he said them that night? He couldn't remember. Three? Five? More?

They'd started in the kitchen. What had she said to him? Something that made him think instantly, *She knows who I really am, she knows what I really feel, she's fabulous. Why didn't I see any of this before?* Within ten minutes they lost all awareness of what was happening around them—the music, the laughter, the people coming and going in search of ice or chips or more beer.

The emotional nakedness and physical hunger between them was wonderful and crippling at the same time. He ached for her, wanted to kiss her and take her to bed so badly, and yet he wanted to listen to her, too. He wasn't simply possessed by a young man's hormonal imperatives, his whole heart was melting and singing. He had no idea it was possible to feel this way. Had no idea how thoroughly they'd already come to know each other after six years as fellow students. Had no idea how he'd failed to see it coming.

It was a warm night, summer just started, air fresh and a little salty because they were near the ocean. 'Want to find somewhere outside?' he asked her, and she nodded. They sat on some brick steps, knees hunched up, bodies touching.

He remembered the sweet smell of flowers. Jasmine, or something. All tangled and lush around the posts and lintel of some wooden white-painted garden arch. It gave them privacy. He kissed her for minutes on end and when he finally pulled away, she smiled into his face and stroked his jaw with her hands, looking at him with a helpless frown on her face as well as the smile, as if, like him, she couldn't understand how something could simultaneously be so strange and so right.

'Dad?' Josh said tentatively, bringing Nick's focus crashing back to the present.

'Yes, lit—? Yes, mate?' Again, he'd almost said *little guy*.

He didn't like *mate*. It didn't feel right. What else was there? *Love. Sweetheart. Darling*. Not those either. He hated it that his son was five years old and he didn't know how to find the right affectionate nickname.

'Can I please have a snack?'

'Sure.' There should be a snack cart coming along soon, but Nick wasn't going to rely on Josh liking airline food. He was absurdly grateful at the mere fact that his son had spoken to him. 'You want the muesli bar or the cheese dipper?'

'Muesli bar.'

'And something to drink?'

'Just water.' He sounded good now, no wheeze left at all.

Miranda appeared. 'If you need the bathroom, now would be a good time, Joshie. Before the aisle gets blocked by the food service.'

Joshie, Nick thought. That worked. That he could say, without feeling that he was somehow faking his way through it.

Thank you, Miranda Carlisle. Again…

They must have talked and kissed and sat on those steps until two or three in the morning, learning about each other, by which time the party had been sagging and ebbing into the usual late night dark kind of feeling, people leaving in twos and threes, warm bodies slumped together on the couch, a touch-and-go moment when an irritable neighbour might have called the police, only someone shut down the pounding music just in time.

'Where could we go?' he asked. 'I want to be with you. I don't think I ever want to let you go.'

He meant it, at the time, more than he'd ever meant anything in his life. Lord, in hindsight the nakedness of it still brought hints of blind panic.

'My place,' she offered at once. It was a shared house. Fellow med students, but they'd gone north to the Gold Coast, she said, for their version of this end-of-exams party night.

Miranda made it clear that the two of them would be alone—a typical gesture of giving, he thought. No one to overhear, no one to hide from, no one to ever know, no matter how late they slept in.

You're safe, Nick.

He knew he never would have made himself that vulnerable, offering 'my place' as if it was the easiest thing in the world. He protected his own space like it was some kind of dark secret, even though it was nothing out of the ordinary, just a ground-level studio flat next to the garage, beneath his landlord's suburban home.

The way he'd protected his heart until that night, with her.

When a dam broke, it flooded…

They made love.

He still remembered odd details. They stood out in his mind like bits of coloured glass catching the sun. Miranda's dark hair sweeping across his chest—it had been longer back then. Her laugh, all creamy and secret and just for him. The confessions he'd made afterwards, while they'd lain in each other's arms until morning, not sleeping at all.

Those confessions had felt liberating at the time, a huge weight off his mind, gateway to a new freedom he hadn't imagined before. 'I'm not sure if I care enough about people to be a good doctor. I have the medicine down, but how do you care the right amount?' 'I don't think I really love my parents the way I should. My father is so…so rigid, and my mother gives in to everyone.' 'Stupidity makes me angry. And weakness. And sneakiness. All those things. I pull back. I just don't deal with it. Is that showing strength, to pull back? Or am I being weak, too?'

He wondered now, as Miranda jumped up once more from the narrow aircraft seat beside him, if she was still as calmly trusting, if she still wore her heart on her sleeve, if she ever said *I love you* the very first night.

He didn't.

He never had since.

Where was the sense in making yourself that vulnerable? he'd decided. And yet holding back, the way he had in his marriage to Anna, hadn't brought him happiness. With any luck, she wouldn't be seated beside him on the next flight—the final hop out to Wallaby Island, on a propeller-driven plane.

As the larger jet flight began its descent into Cairns, the 'Fasten Seat Belt' sign confined Miranda in place and she felt so aware of Nick—the forbidding silence broken only by occasional rather wooden comments to Josh, the strong shoulder that encroached a little into her own space. Hadn't these airline seats grown even smaller and more cramped since the last time she'd flown?

It was so stupid. She really wanted to say to him, *So why did you never phone me, when you promised that you would?* After ten years, you just didn't ask that. After ten years, you already knew.

There were basically only two possibilities.

Either he had only wanted to get her into bed, and hadn't minded lying to her for the sake of that goal. *'I love you, Miranda.'*

Or in the cold light of day, he hadn't found her nearly as captivating as the party in the moonlight had led him to think.

At the time, she'd believed his sincerity absolutely, hadn't even thought to take his phone number as insurance. He had said he would phone, he had said he loved her, which meant he would and did, so she hadn't needed his number. When a day went by, then two, then a week, the pain and questions started to slow-burn inside her and lasted for months.

Had she completely misread that sense of rightness and promise? Why had she trusted him so easily?

Because, despite her stellar performance in her studies, she had been as dumb as a rock in some areas, and one of those areas was men. There was a causal link to the apparent contradiction. She had been clueless when it had come to men *because* she'd done so well in her studies.

Success in medicine took hard work. Hard work left little time for other activities. Other activities included hanging out with female friends, meeting men and talking about the men in great detail with the female friends.

She'd been the beloved only child of older parents. She'd grown up too sheltered and too eager to give her heart. She honestly hadn't known that some men were love rats, and that you couldn't always tell who the love rats were at first—or even second or third—glance. Shutting herself away to study, she hadn't had enough opportunity to experience the bruising reality of the real world. She'd stayed far too innocent for far too long. Was probably too innocent still. Too innocent and too nice. How did you get tougher? Did she want to? She hadn't realised that matters of the heart required as much prior study as an anatomy exam.

Oh, and there was another reason why she'd believed the *I love you* thing.

Because she'd said the same words back to him, all night, and had meant them from the bottom of her heart.

'Joshie, we need to put the cars away now, so we can put your tray table up,' Nick said to his son.

No reply.

'Josh, are you listening?'

'Is this the kids' camp?' He twisted around for a moment, and might have been talking to

Miranda, not to his dad. She felt Nick stiffen beside her, and stayed silent, leaving the conversation to unfold between father and son, the way it should. 'I can see buildings. They're tiny!'

'No, this isn't the camp,' Nick answered, 'because we have to go on the other plane first, remember? That's Cairns you can see.'

'And I can see ocean and sand, and shapes in the water.'

'Let me look…' Nick leaned past Josh. 'Wow!'

The aircraft banked to line up its approach and Miranda caught a glimpse of tropical yellow and blue, sun glinting on water, and lush rainforest greenery. The promise of the water, the warmth and the reef washed over her like a delectable scent in the air and for a moment she had absolute faith that they were all going to have a great time.

She was too adept at faith, though, too nice for her own good.

Hold back, Miranda. Keep your heart safe. Haven't you learned that yet?

Well, if she hadn't, she had Nick Devlin on hand to remind her.

CHAPTER THREE

'RIGHT, that's everything on file,' Dr Beth Stuart said to Miranda. 'Your lot and Benita's. She'll be along in a minute, you said.'

'She's still getting her group settled. I won't be surprised if it takes a while.'

'Well, we won't wait for her. I'll show you our set-up, and you probably have questions, Miranda.'

'At the moment, I'm too impressed to think of them! Speechless, really.'

'I know. It's pretty fantastic, isn't it? Charles says it's an ill wind—' Beth interrupted herself. 'That's Charles Wetherby, Medical Director, I mean. You'll meet him. Soon, I expect. He said he'd pop in, and if not he'll be at dinner in the camp dining room.' She looked at her watch. 'Only an hour away. Time's getting on.'

'He lives out here? I thought—'

'He's based in Crocodile Creek, yes, on the

mainland. But this place is his baby, administratively part of the Crocodile Creek Hospital, and he pushed through the rebuilding after the cyclone with amazing speed. That's what he meant about the ill wind. It took a cyclone to get a state-of-the-art medical centre here, but now it means we can take kids for the camp that we couldn't have taken in the past because their health was too iffy for us to handle.'

'Were you here when the cyclone hit?'

'No, I've only been working here for a few weeks.'

Miranda matched this statement with Beth's use of the word 'we.' Clearly she'd settled in and become attached to the place very fast. She was a slightly built woman in her thirties, with typical brunette colouring, hair kept practical and straight and chin length.

'I live in one of the old camp cabins that survived the cyclone. Somewhat primitive but that's fine. It's supposed to be a temporary arrangement, but I might start kicking and screaming if they try to move me somewhere supposedly better. There's something about this place, and my little cabin. Good for the soul. And

I love the kids!' A bright grin came and went, showing a different side to her personality.

Beth seemed outgoing at first glance, but Miranda wondered about the stream of easy chat. Was there more beneath the surface? In her experience, there usually was. Most women, once they'd passed thirty, had a challenge or two behind them.

'They didn't used to have a full-time doctor on staff,' Beth was saying. 'The medical centre was much more modest, but now we're effectively a hospital and I'm the doctor who runs it.'

'Not on your own?'

'No, we roster people across from Crocodile Creek. Charles himself. He's the one I report to, officially. Dr Jamieson, Dr Lopez. Several others. You'll meet some of them. Oh, this is him, I think.'

Miranda hadn't heard anything. But then the door opened as if by magic—no, by a little girl, she saw a moment later—and a man in a wheel-chair manoeuvred his way through, followed by a woolly, goldy-brown dog. He smiled at her—the man, not the dog—and they did the whole greetings and introductions thing.

'And the dog is Garf,' Charles finished.

'Garf is gorgeous. What breed?'

'Labradoodle. They're good for the asthma kids because they don't shed. He's six years old.' Charles looked to be somewhere in his late forties or fifties, greying slightly at the temples, with lines deepening at the corners of his well-shaped mouth and serious-yet-twinkly dark eyes. The little girl was Lily, but where she fitted into the picture neither Charles nor Beth explained.

Charles seemed preoccupied. 'We have dignitaries descending from Tuesday onwards for the official opening,' he was saying, 'and I have—' He stopped, looked at Lily.

Lily was busy linking all the paper clips from the tray on the desk into a long silver chain. Much more interesting than listening to adult conversation.

'Can you watch Lily for a minute, Beth? Unless…' He looked at Miranda. 'We're staying in one of the camp cabins until after the opening. Dinner's up soon. Would you be able to take Lily across with you, Dr Carlisle, and I'll meet you there a little later on?'

'Of course,' Miranda told him politely. 'But would she…um…?'

'Go with you?' he mouthed back, understanding her hesitation. He murmured, 'Yes, almost too easily. Jill and I worry about it.' Charles turned to the child. 'Lily, you're going to go with Dr Carlisle and meet all the camp kids. That'll be much more fun than coming to the hotel.'

Lily nodded and dropped her paper-clip chain. She darted ahead of Charles so she could open the office door for him.

'Be good for Dr Carlisle, won't you?' he said. 'Make friends with the camp kids.'

'Can I take Garf?'

'No, I'd better have him with me,' Charles told her. 'See you later, OK?'

He manoevred himself out the door and down the wheelchair ramp that ran across the front of the brand-new building, and a moment later man and woolly golden dog were out of sight.

'Lily, ready to go with Dr Carlisle?' Beth asked.

Lily nodded.

Miranda thought about suggesting the use of her first name, but her patients didn't call her that, so she probably shouldn't offer the informality to Lily either. She said a see-you-around kind of goodbye to Beth and left the brand-new building. Lily knew the way to go. She skipped on ahead, while Miranda tried to orientate herself.

They passed some of the original cabins, which had been left sufficiently intact to warrant repairing after the cyclone. Two of them had had their windows left unglazed and seemed to have been fitted out for pottery and painting. The third cabin, set slightly behind the first two, must be Beth's. Miranda glimpsed nests of colourful cushions on a squishy old couch and saw rows of shells and other beachcomber bric-a-brac arranged on the veranda railing. The place must have the most gorgeous views of the ocean...

Farther along, camouflaged by the tropical greenery, which was already recovering well from the cyclone's damage, were the newly built eco-cabins and camp dormitories, as well as the dining hall and activity rooms. Lily pricked up her ears at the sound of children's voices, and Miranda saw a couple of departing parents being ferried by electric golf cart down to the luxury hotel resort on the other side of the island. Not all of the accompanying parents had elected to stay at the camp itself.

Nick was staying here, though.

He and Josh had one of the two-bedroom cabins set off to the far side of the cluster of camp buildings. Miranda saw them come out onto their veranda. Josh was holding himself apart, fiddling with something he'd picked up. Probably a shell. He didn't look at Nick. His little legs looked so thin and small below a pair of baggy blue shorts.

Nick watched him and didn't seem to know what to say. He looked tense and awkward and that phrase *love rat* that had come into her head earlier didn't seem to fit him at all. 'Don't you want to, Josh?' Miranda heard him say. 'There's time.'

No reply.

'Listen, you have to talk to me, or I don't know what you want. Go to the beach before dinner? Or stay here? Are you too hungry? Thirsty?'

Josh caught sight of Miranda at that moment. He grinned and clambered down the wooden steps, still without having given his father an answer. 'Can we go to the beach?'

'I think your dad just said you could, didn't he?' She could see Nick's feet planted firmly on the wooden veranda as if something had frozen him there. He looked forbidding and not happy, and she didn't want to say or do the wrong thing. 'I think Dad wants to scrunch some sand between his toes,' she finished lightly.

'Are you going?' Josh asked her, his gaze steady on her face.

Miranda didn't know. She had Lily to consider, and Charles Wetherby hadn't mentioned taking the little girl to the beach.

Beside her, Lily took matters into her own hands. 'Yep, we're going. Look, it's right there.' Without waiting for any further guidance from the adults, she set off. Nick and Miranda exchanged glances. Josh was looking much happier than he had a minute ago. He scampered in Lily's wake, and Nick and Miranda accepted their fate and followed.

'This one's not from the Melbourne group, is she?' Nick asked.

'No, she's from here. She belongs to Dr Wetherby, I think.'

'Belongs to him?'

'I haven't quite worked their relationship out,' Miranda confessed.

'I know how that feels,' he muttered.

She was about to question the statement, but he didn't give her a chance. As if wanting to create some distance, he quickened his pace to catch up to the two kids, which meant that Miranda took her first steps onto the beach alone.

It was glorious.

A wide, shallow curve of white sand cupped the tropical water like a rim of fine porcelain. The colour of the ocean was fantastic, shading from light turquoise in the shallows through aquamarine and peacock to a rich, satiny midnight blue out where it was deeper.

Miranda glimpsed a scattering of smaller islands to the left and right, and there were a couple of boats anchored off a rocky point. They bobbed lazily in the blue, and she could see people on deck, sunbathing or sitting back with cool drinks in their hands. Behind the beach rose the island.

Going further out onto the sand, she could look back and get a better sense of the place than she had during their descent in the plane over an hour ago. A couple of the kids had been queasy at that point and she'd barely managed a glance out of the windows. The island was bigger, wilder and more rugged than she'd expected, rising to a rainforest-covered peak in the centre, with all sorts of hidden gullies and slopes.

The resort at the south end and the camp at the north both had only narrow toeholds on the place, linked by a couple of service roads and walking trails that skirted the steeper slopes and stuck close to the water.

Standing transfixed by the peace and beauty of it all, as the sun began its rapid late afternoon drop towards the horizon, Miranda wanted someone beside her who could share the moment but, as so often seemed to happen, she was on her own.

Not that the beach was deserted. Several families had already made their way down here, and Benita was here, too, with a group of the older kids who'd come to camp without their parents.

They'd hit rip-roaring adolescence, some of them. Miranda saw a giggling teenage girl, her body puffy from medication side-effects, enjoying a mock sword fight with a curly-haired boy Miranda knew that she herself would have considered drop-dead cute at fourteen—the surfer type, all salty blond hair and tanned limbs and newly deepened voice. He was one of the in-remission cancer kids, she thought, and he had a natural, infectious smile.

Stella sat on the sand with her crutches beside her, her prosthesis still hidden by jeans, socks and athletic shoes, and her chemotherapy hair covered by a backward-facing baseball cap shoved firmly on her head. Pretty and fragile blonde Lauren Allandale, whose spoiled only-child status was hugely exacerbated by her parents' understandable concern over her cystic fibrosis, was standing with her mum and dad, staring disdainfully at Stella—without the latter seeing, thank goodness—as if to say, *This* is the friendship material I have to work with? Tell me there's someone else!

The two girls were almost the same age, but poles apart in most other ways, it seemed. Lauren was tiny and frail-looking. Portable oxygen equipment stood on the sand beside her, and a wheelchair sat on the wooden boardwalk, ready for when she had tired herself out and needed to rest. She had recently been put on the lung transplant list, while Stella hopefully had the worst of her cancer treatment behind her.

Stella passionately hated what had happened to her, whereas at some level, having lived with CF all her life, Lauren had learned to trade on her poor health, even to value it in an upside-down way. It gave her a certain status, and an excuse for her spoiled-brat behaviour. Miranda found her a difficult patient, but privately considered that her parents' doting attitude hadn't done her any favours.

Both girls had faced more than their fair share of challenges, but so far this common ground didn't look as if it would turn them into friends. It was a pity, given what Benita had said about Stella needing someone to be close to.

Now was not the right time to try and bridge the obvious distance between the girls, Miranda decided.

She took several automatic steps in the direction of Lily, Josh and Nick, instead, but then she slowed her pace and stopped. Lily had latched onto Nick like a favourite uncle. 'Dig here,' she ordered him, taking it for granted that she had him wrapped around her little finger already. 'Deep, so the water comes in.'

'Yes, boss,' Nick drawled, laughing.

The laughter still suited him, although Miranda had the impression it remained as rare as it had been in his student days. It turned his cool smile into a wide grin, showed his white teeth and created a rich sound from low in his diaphragm. He got down on his hands and knees and began to dig, crawling around in his navy shorts and polo shirt as if there was nothing in the world he wanted more than to be excavating holes on a tropical beach.

Josh hung back, however, watching the interaction between his father and the little girl as though he was waiting for something to explode.

Nick was quick to notice his son's distance. 'Want to help me, Joshie?' he invited cheerfully, sitting up on his haunches.

No answer.

'Joshie, we have to collect things to decorate the pool,' ordered Lily, and to that Josh nodded. He began the task at once, running over the sand, picking up shells and bits of seaweed and broken coral, seeming immediately bright, eager and involved.

Until Nick spoke to him again. 'How about a tunnel here at the end? I'll dig another hole so we have two pools with a bridge over the top?'

Josh pretended not to hear. 'Look at this shell, Lily.'

Nick kept digging, face hidden as he bent into the rapidly deepening hole.

Miranda didn't know what to do. She could see exactly what was going on and all her instincts told her that Nick minded terribly about his son's awkward rejection, but, oh, she couldn't let him get under her skin this fast, couldn't care this much.

It was the same old pattern that he'd been responsible for in the first place. Friends, colleagues, family, patients…all those relationships worked fine, it was safe to give and she was good at it, but when it came to matters of love, she was so afraid of giving her heart away too soon that, since Nick, she had never given it away at all.

Her ex-boyfriend, Ian Mackenzie, had probably deserved more.

A couple of other parents and kids had questions or just wanted to chat, so she did that. She talked about what she'd seen at the new medical centre, promised to clear up a couple of details with the camp staff later on, assured the Allandales that she had the physiotherapy appointment schedule back in her cabin and would let people know their times over dinner.

She saw Stella and Lauren both looking surreptitiously at the salt-blond surfer boy—Jamie, she'd heard someone call him—and immediately thought, Uh-oh, there's some hormonal trouble brewing!

For ten minutes she carried on various conversations with one part of her mind, while watching Nick and his son with the rest, wondering if she should interfere, step in and try to ease their uncomfortable dealings with each other if she could, or if, once more, she would simply be her own worst enemy.

Nick sat back on his heels, finally. 'There!'

The sand construction was magnificent. Two paddling pools connected by a square-sided canal that ran beneath a bridge cut into the sand. Josh smiled at the whole thing and Nick seemed to drink in the expression on his son's face the way a thirsty man drank fresh water.

Too soon, however, disaster struck.

Josh didn't realise that the bridge only held itself together through the damp, compacted consistency of the sand. It wouldn't bear any weight. Before Nick understood the little boy's intention, he'd put a foot square in the middle of it and it collapsed under him. There was no damage to Josh, but the neat little sand structure was ruined.

Josh threw a terror-stricken look at his father and stood ankle deep in wet sand, frozen, waiting for the blow to fall. 'I'm sorry,' he whispered, the words dragging out of him.

'It's OK, Joshie, it's fine,' Nick said quickly, his voice rising in pitch as he sought to reassure his son. 'I should have warned you the sand wasn't strong enough. It's not your fault, OK?'

The indomitable Lily yelled, 'Let's build it again!' and got to work at once, in a doomed attempt to create a sand arch over the collapse.

But Josh wasn't interested any more. Or else he didn't trust the way his dad had reacted. Was the anger yet to come? he seemed to be wondering. He wandered off silently, towards the water. Nick's gaze followed him, while every muscle on his strong frame had gone rigid.

Looking on, Miranda could read the body language in both of them like a book and she couldn't bear it. She felt a sudden spurt of anger against Anna Devlin that shocked her. Nick had his faults as a father and as a man but he would have to have a black heart indeed to deserve what Anna had done, whether deliberately or unconsciously, to his relationship with his son.

Josh was scared of him.

He didn't know him, and he didn't trust him, and Anna had communicated to the child all her own bitterness and soured love, her doubts about Nick's abilities as a father, her fear that she was the only one who understood his asthma well enough, her over-emotional reactions to everything Nick said or did, and it just wasn't fair.

It put Nick in an agonising position here at the camp, and for a few stark moments every bit of that agony showed in his face.

Without quite knowing how she'd got there, Miranda found herself at Nick's side. 'You'll have to be patient,' she blurted out.

She put a hand on his bare upper arm, but that felt too much like an invasion of his space. He hadn't invited the gesture, and his knotted muscle hadn't softened to accept it. He'd always been very good at maintaining physical distance when he wanted to. Bare feet planted apart, gaze fixed on the horizon, body brown and big and strong, and saying loud and clear, *Don't touch me.*

She took her hand away, but just as she did so he softened a little and half turned to her, palms open and upward in a gesture of appeal. 'We have a week,' he said. 'A bare week. What is it they say in the tourist brochures? Six days, seven nights. I don't think it's enough. Not anywhere near.'

'It's a long time in a child's life. Especially in a place like this.'

'It's not a long time in mine. It's way too short.' His voice was low and emotional. No one else would hear this. It was meant only for her, and she somehow knew that her timing had been perfect. Too perfect. She'd caught him at a moment of vulnerability that was very rare indeed. 'To bridge all that distance? To wipe those shuttered, fearful expressions from his face when he looks at me? I hadn't realised until today that it was this bad. Oh, in my heart, I suppose I knew, but...'

'No, that's not how he—'

'Yes. It is how he looks at me. Don't pretend. I'm sure you can see it.'

'Sometimes kids get it wrong,' she said inadequately.

He ignored her. 'I want this week so much. It seemed like the answer to a prayer. So help me, my mother-in-law is not a bad woman, I shouldn't applaud her broken leg, but I did. I do. Anna would never have let me have this time with him if there'd been another option, if Josh hadn't been looking forward to the camp so much and if she'd had even a day longer to make alternative plans. I can only imagine how close she came to cancelling Josh's stay altogether rather than having him come here with me. This close.' He pressed his right thumb and forefinger together, leaving a minute sliver of space.

'Nick, you don't—'

He seemed to read her thoughts. 'You're right. I don't know for sure she was thinking that way. But I do know for a fact that she phoned both her sisters first to see if either of them could look after their mother or bring Josh up here. They'd have had to fly up separately. They're in Sydney.

But she would have preferred that—having him fly up on his own to meet an aunt he doesn't know very well. I was most definitely the last resort. A week is a tiny amount of time. Unless he's miserable here, miserable with *me*, in which case it's going to feel like seven years of hell.'

'How did this happen, Nick? What went wrong?'

'How long have you got?' he countered bitterly.

No time at all, as it turned out. A siren sounded, and Miranda knew it was the call to dinner, which she suspected wouldn't exactly be the most private hour of the day for her, here at the camp, given her professional role.

'Let's go, everybody!' she called out, waving her hands in the air. Not everybody knew yet what the siren meant. 'Lily, Lauren, Stella, everybody. Dinner's up. Let's find out what the food is like.' She dropped her voice again and began to pivot around. 'Nick, why don't we try to meet up later and—?'

But he wasn't there.

He'd turned away from her to walk down to the frilly little waves at the water's edge, where Josh stood. Taking his son's hand, he said in a neutral voice, 'Dinnertime, Joshie, come on.' And the two of them walked up the beach together a yard and a half apart, with fingers tenuously and uncomfortably joined.

CHAPTER FOUR

WHY had he dumped all that stuff about his relationship with Josh on Miranda, of all people?

Nick felt almost ill about it—restless and wound
up and helpless, bitterly regretful of his own loss
of emotional control, the way he'd felt after their
night together ten years ago. You just shouldn't do
things like that. Why? Where did it get you?

They'd managed to get through dinner, he and
Josh, without any huge problems. No traces of
egg or nuts in the food to trigger one of Josh's
allergies. No accidental spills. He'd eaten with
hearty enthusiasm, which always gave Nick an
irrational degree of pleasure.

But there'd been the usual distance between
them. Josh had stayed largely silent, watching a
couple of the other kids talking and laughing.
He'd responded minimally to anything Nick
said. Nick had had to ask Josh twice to pass him

the pepper before he'd paid any attention and when he had, it had just been with the action. No 'There you are, Dad,' or even 'OK.' Lily was sitting next to a man in a wheelchair—her father, presumably—on the far side of the big dining room, which was a pity because the two kids had done so well together on the beach.

Josh was tired, that was part of it. Back at the cabin, he had a quick bath and his night-time regimen of preventative asthma treatment and breathing exercises, and then he fell asleep barely halfway through the Greedy Frog story Nick read to him.

All good, except that it was only just after seven-thirty, which left Nick with a solid three hours before his own bedtime—a huge window of opportunity for regretting every word of what he'd said to Miranda on the beach.

These eco-cabins didn't have TV. Nick had now read through every page of the information folder he'd found. And he'd packed in too much of a hurry this morning to remember to bring a book of his own, while the plot line in Josh's Very Greedy Frog story just wasn't gripping enough to the adult mind to sustain a second reading! He would need to raid the resort gift shop for a couple of nice thick paperbacks tomorrow, or Josh's early bedtimes would become very limiting by the end of the week.

Or maybe Joshie could manage a late nap during the day, he decided after some more thought, and then the two of them could take part in the evening activities listed on the schedule. The torch-lit night-time walks in search of nocturnal animals, the kids' disco on Friday night as part of the opening celebrations, the campfire supper.

It was a plan, but it didn't help Nick right now.

He couldn't leave Josh alone in the cabin, but he felt too restless and dissatisfied with himself to stay inside. Instead, he made a mug of decaf, black with one sugar, and went out onto the veranda, where at least the sense of vague claustrophobia should lessen.

It was a gorgeous night, the air soft and buttery and salt-flavoured, filled with the rhythmic washing sound of the sea. He sat in one of the veranda's big, cushion-covered wicker chairs and sipped his coffee, hoping that the air and the sounds would soothe his unsettled, regretful state.

They didn't.

What would Miranda think?

He couldn't let it go. Never had been able to let that kind of thing go, the rare times when it had happened—just twice, really, in his whole adult life. His night with Miranda had been the second time, and the night of his father's death the first. That time, thank goodness, the urgent sounding of a monitor alarm had saved him from spilling everything to the soft-voiced, sympathetic nurse with the warm eyes who'd been at his father's deathbed, when nineteen-year-old Nick himself had missed his father's final moments by just half an hour. The alarm had cut him off a few minutes in, before any tears had come—before he'd literally cried on the nurse's shoulder.

Dad himself would have been relieved. He had taught all three of his sons—Nick was the eldest—to present a strong and inviolate front to the world. Never show your deep emotions or your doubts. Never admit when you're wrong. Don't let people discover your Achilles' heel or they'll use it against you.

For a successful surgeon, the strategy worked.

For a man struggling after a divorce, fighting to keep and build a relationship with his only child...

He honestly didn't know any more.

Hell, what would Miranda think of him now?

What kind of a man inspired fear and distance in his own son? What kind of a man admitted to it, in a truncated semi-public conversation with a woman he hadn't seen in ten years?

Why was Miranda's effect on him still the same? Something about her. Something about the indefinable chemistry between them. It was a long way from being just physical. For some unaccountable reason, she shattered his barriers just by being who she was. He could *talk* to her in a way he'd never talked to anyone else.

He'd first discovered his connection to Miranda at that medical students' party ten years ago and the dam inside him had burst open. The next day he'd felt exactly the way he was feeling now, regret souring his stomach and tightening like an iron band around his head.

Why the hell had he let it happen? Why had he said so much? What would she think? Lord, he'd been so naked in what he'd said! She must think less of him because of it. She must! What red-blooded woman wanted an emotional, self-doubting wimp in her life?

It was like going into battle with no armour. Like swimming naked in a pool of sharks. Not just dangerous, plain stupid.

That was how his thinking had run at the age of twenty-four.

That was why he'd never phoned her after that long-ago night.

Because he had been too scared. Because he just hadn't imagined that she would want him to continue what they'd started after he'd shown himself to be so weak, and because he couldn't bring himself to risk that vulnerability again, even if she did.

What the hell might he tell her in the future? he'd wondered ten years ago.

About the times he'd cried himself to sleep at fourteen and even sixteen, in sheer impotent frustration, after some angry, circular altercation with his father? About how competitive he'd been with his medical studies, so that the prospect of anything less than stellar results had filled him with physical dread? About the secret, appalling thread of *relief* he'd felt at nineteen when Dad had died, mingling so painfully with his grief?

It was destructive and pointless to shine a light on that stuff. You shouldn't dwell on your failings and weaknesses. That wasn't the way to overcome them.

Words had power.

When you talked about something, you made it more real.

Now, almost in his mid-thirties, he intellectually understood that talking could sometimes help. Lord knew, he'd tried to talk to Anna when their marriage had begun to break down and many times since then, but they always seemed to hear the wrong things in what each other said, and their talks frequently made things worse, not better. Their relationship had never held that kind of intimacy and shared nakedness.

It was one of things he'd considered a strength at the time. Now he was a lot less sure. And yet the regret about talking to Miranda remained…

He must have been sitting out on the cabin porch for over an hour by this time.

He heard various sounds above the musical play of the ocean. Kid sounds, mainly—bumps and scramblings and noise and giggling, inter-spersed with the occasional adult voice. Lights flipped on and off in various windows. Clattering and more voices came from the camp kitchen where cleaning up was still in progress, as well as advance preparations for tomorrow's meals.

Then, out of the darkness, he heard women's voices and laughter, approaching from the direc-tion of the medical centre.

Apparently even *thinking* about certain things could make them more real. He'd been thinking about Miranda and what she'd done to him ten years ago and now, and magically here she was, appearing in silhouette as she came along the mulched path with Susie Jackson, the camp physiotherapist he'd been introduced to briefly over dinner.

From the way they were talking, it sounded as if they'd already made friends and he had time to wonder how it was that women could *do* that. So quickly and easily giving themselves. As if it wasn't scary at all. How did they latch on so fast to the points of connection? How could they tell so quickly who to trust?

'We'll give it a try tomorrow,' he heard Susie say. Then the two women said a warm, cheerful goodnight to each other and Susie peeled off in a different direction while Miranda came past Nick's cabin.

She saw him, of course. He was sitting in front of the main window, and he'd left a light on in the cabin's kitchenette in case Josh woke up and became disorientated in unfamiliar surroundings. The light spilled through the window and showed Nick's position on the veranda quite clearly, leaving no opportunity to hide.

'Hi,' she said.

'Hi. Everything OK?'

'It's fine.' She came to a hesitant halt, and Nick could see her wondering if this was a whole conversation or just a greeting on the move. 'Susie did a couple of evening physio sessions on my CF patients and I wanted to be on hand this first night. Then we sat and talked for a while. No dramas, thank goodness. Pager hasn't gone off.' She patted her hip pocket.

'Sounds good,' he said mechanically, willing her to keep walking.

His neck had gone hot. She must be thinking

about what he'd said on the beach. She *must*. And he didn't want her to. He wanted her to forget the conversation had ever happened.

He struggled to find something else to say, something that would dismiss her and send her on her way without the fact being too obvious, but the right words refused to come. The silence stretched out. Two or three seconds could feel like that many minutes in a situation like this.

'Did you—?' he began, just as she spoke at last, breezy and offhand.

'Well, have a good night, Nick.'

'You, too.'

She walked on and he started to relax. She'd saved him, thank goodness, from uttering an inane line about whether she'd remembered to bring a book, because if she hadn't he could recommend a great story about a Very Greedy Frog, ha, ha.

He watched her go, her hips swaying slightly beneath a fall of swishy fabric in the same colours as that spectacular ocean just a hundred metres away, her shoulders neat and square on either side of her bouncing ponytail of dark hair. She looked about nineteen years old, although he knew full well that she was thirty-four, and he had a sudden surge of intense curiosity about what her life was like these days.

He was pretty sure she wasn't married…boyfriend, maybe…and quite sure she didn't have kids. But she did have a balcony where she kept plants. He couldn't even remember how he knew that ridiculous detail, he just did.

It wasn't enough.

Eight-thirty in the evening, on his own, nothing to do, with Miranda disturbing his thoughts for another hour, probably, even if she wasn't physically present…

Damn.

'Miranda, wait!' he called out, just before she disappeared into the darkness on the way to her own cabin.

Miranda stopped. Right at the point when she'd absolutely made up her mind that Nick really didn't want her to stay and chat, he was calling her back.

So what should she do about it? How much pride did she have? How nice was she? Once again, it hadn't been hard to pick up his body language as he sat on the veranda. He'd struggled for something to say. He hadn't stood up or anything, hadn't tried to draw out their conversation, or even really looked at her face.

She knew a little more about men than she'd known ten years ago. She'd been with Ian for six years, after all, even though for three of those years it had been a long-distance thing. If a man wanted to talk—or even spend time with you in silence—he was usually pretty good at letting you know it. He closed the physical distance between the two of you. He looked directly at you. He smiled.

Nick hadn't done any of those things.

Was this an issue of her pride, though, or was there another possibility?

'I should probably go and relax for a while,' she said, coming slowly back. Was this really what he wanted? Or, for both their sakes, should she give him an easy way out?

'Relax here,' he invited her. 'I can't leave Josh or take him anywhere, he's fast asleep. Wish I could offer you some wine.'

'I wouldn't take it. I'm pretty much on call for the kids all week.' She arrived at the short flight of wooden steps that led up to the veranda.

'Not a holiday for you, then.'

'Not really.' She smiled at him, to see if he'd smile back. 'Although I do have high hopes for my tan…' Nope. No smile.

'Please, come and sit,' he repeated, and this time he jumped to his feet almost eagerly and dragged the veranda's second chair into a more inviting position, as if he really meant it.

'Just a few minutes,' she said, making a point of looking at her watch so that she could claim another commitment if necessary.

She honestly didn't know if she was being pathetic, stepping onto his veranda. Too nice, as usual. Too happy to give.

Damn it, though! She hated the way some people told you to play games in a relationship. Don't show your emotional cards until you've seen his. Play hard to get. If you began a relationship with games, at what point did you stop them? Patterns were hard to break once you'd set them up. She'd kept her emotional cards to her chest with Ian. It had gone against everything in her nature, and it hadn't led to a happy ending, had it? Wasn't simple honesty the better approach? Honesty to the person you were with, and honesty to yourself about your own nature.

We're adults, Nick and I, she reminded herself. We're in our thirties, successful professionally, with a divorce under his belt and a failed long-term relationship under mine. I can step onto his veranda without it saying anything about what happened ten years ago.

'You're frowning,' he said.

'Didn't mean to.'

'Want some tea or coffee?'

'Tea, please. Just a quick cup.' Mugs could be handy things to look down at when you didn't want to meet somebody's eyes.

He rose at once and went inside, and she heard the sounds he made in the kitchen. In a few minutes he'd returned, the cardboard tea-bag tag still dangling over the edge of the mug, which was one of those ubiquitous pearlescent orange ones she remembered from her childhood, and even then they hadn't been new.

Handing it to her, Nick said, 'This must be a cyclone survivor, I think. My aunt and uncle had a cupboard full of these at their beach house.'

She laughed. 'I was thinking almost the same

thing. My parents had rows of them, twenty-five years ago, hanging on hooks on the wall.'

'The camp has been here in some form or other for donkey's years, I gather.'

'Not always for kids like our lot, though.'

'No. A church camp, then a nudist colony, in the eighties. Long ago, they used to hunt mutton birds on the island, for their oil.'

'You've done your research!'

'That's what teachers used to say on my school reports.' He quoted self-mockingly, 'Nick is always well prepared.'

'I'm seriously wondering how you knew this place was once a nudist colony, let alone about the mutton bird oil.'

'No great mystery. My son was fast asleep by seven twenty-five, and I forgot to pack a book to read in the evenings. As a piece of gripping literature, the Crocodile Creek Kids' Camp information folder provided a somewhat disappointing alternative, but the page on the camp's history was pure gold.'

'Oh, let me lend you a book, then. I optimistically packed three.' She named them—one chunky piece of crime fiction, one delectably fluffy beach read and one literary novel. She almost added, Only keep your hands off my beach read, because I want that one first!

He chose the murder mystery, and looked much more cheerful than he had a few minutes ago. She promised him, 'I'll grab it from my cabin in a minute.'

'Tomorrow at breakfast will be fine. For the rest of the week, I'm going to try to get Josh to have an afternoon sleep so we can do some of the evening stuff, but that might not work, which will mean I get a lot of bedtime reading done.'

'There's a babysitting service available through the resort hotel's child-care centre. Beth and Susie have both promised me it's very responsible. The centre staff all have formal qualifications in child care, as well as first-aid certificates.'

'I must have missed that detail in the folder. Can't think how, because I really thought I'd read it cover to cover.'

A silence fell.

Miranda felt fine about it, which wasn't always the case when two people didn't know each other very well—which she and Nick surely didn't, any more. She sipped her tea and settled herself more comfortably into the chair, noting the way the soft light from the cabin window emphasised the craggy lines of Nick's profile and the bulk of his shoulders.

His shoulders were tense.

Apparently he wasn't fine about the silence.

'Listen, what I said to you on the beach this afternoon…'

'I know.' She nodded. 'We didn't get a chance to finish. Of course we can talk about it now, Nick, if you want.'

'No, that's not what I meant.' He shifted awkwardly in his seat. 'Look, just forget the whole conversation. I shouldn't have said any of it. It wasn't fair to you or Josh, or— Yeah, not fair to anyone.'

'Not fair to you?' she interposed softly.

'What? Oh, fair to me?' He laughed, a short unhappy sound, and ran a hand up the back of his neck. 'That's hardly the point, is it?'

'Well, don't you think it might be? Nick, we were friends, once.' She couldn't help watching him, wishing she could come closer. Touch him even, the way she'd tried to do on the beach.

Just on his arm. 'We went through medical school together, we—Well... And I'm your son's doctor. I'm not going to betray your confidence, or judge you, or use it against you. If you needed to talk—'

'No, I shouldn't have said it,' he repeated, the stubborn repudiation of his own behaviour—and his own needs?—etched in every line of his body.

After that, there was nowhere to go. She couldn't keep pushing. And she couldn't think of anything else to say that didn't sound like a very forced attempt to change the subject. Neither, apparently, could he.

She ended up gulping her tea too fast and almost burning her throat. When she made I'd-better-go-now noises and got to her feet, he stood too. 'Thanks for keeping me company.'

'Not for long enough. It's still only nine. But I should...' She made a vague gesture in the direction of her cabin.

'You'll probably be busy tomorrow,' he agreed.

'And I could be up in the night with some of the kids. Tayla's prone to night-time asthma attacks. A couple of them need meds at ten.' He must be riveted by that information!

After a few more awkward phrases from both of them, she said goodnight and left him on his own with the thoughts he refused to share, but she wondered if she'd been wrong ten years ago about why he'd never phoned.

Could it possibly be that he'd been too full of regret about how much he'd given of himself that night?

Having retreated to bed at nine-thirty in a state of one part boredom, two parts regret and three parts frustration, Nick woke early the next morning. The sun had not yet risen above the horizon, although he could tell it wouldn't be long.

He dressed quickly in shorts and a T-shirt, wanting to get out into the freshness of the dawn air, but he made too much noise and heard the creak of the bed in Josh's room. He'd woken him. Josh appeared in the doorway, still looking sleepy and confused.

Nick took no time to think and no time to take it slow. Instead, he scooped his son into his arms, still in his little cotton pyjamas, and told him, 'Come on, we're going to watch the sun come up.'

The beach was deserted, the sand still cool and

grey and shaded, and the ocean as flat as glass. This part of the island faced the north-east, and on the far right of the sweeping vista Nick could see the place where the sun would rise. He just had time to set Josh down in front of him, sheltering him from the light chill in the breeze with his own body. 'Feet cold?'

'No.'

'Ever seen the sun rise?'

'In hospital.'

Oh, hell…

He squeezed Josh's shoulders. 'Well, this will be much better.'

It was. Seconds later, a line of fire spread between the sky and the water, which was suddenly dazzling with white light. The air immediately began to warm, while colour spread over everything. The greens of the rainforest glowed. The sand turned to gold. The sky grew bluer and deeper by the minute.

'Can I swim?' Josh asked.

They hadn't brought a towel or a swimsuit, but Nick couldn't turn down the idea. Josh's whole face was eager and his breathing was clear, no hint of a wheeze.

And he's talking to me. He's looking *at me.*

Somehow the looking felt even more important than the talking. He could deal with Josh's silences—just—but the resolute, close-faced looking away always cut him to the bone.

'Sure,' he said. 'Take off your pyjama top and just wear the bottoms.'

He stripped off his own stretch cotton T-shirt, thinking that it could serve as a towel to wrap Josh in if he got cold.

Would he?

Anna had stressed the danger of sudden cold as a trigger for Josh's attacks. Nick hated that she gave him these intimidating lists of warnings and reminders when he would have known it all for himself if she hadn't tried so hard to keep him away.

As usual, he questioned his own degree of blame. He had withdrawn too much. He hadn't fought hard enough. He'd let her shut him out. The two of them had got married for the wrong reasons, and that fact hadn't helped. When the emotions had got tough, he'd opted out. Had he learned this lesson from his father too well? Was he wrong?

The air wasn't cold, he decided.

They went down to the water together. Josh loved swimming in the heated pool he went to every week. Most asthmatics were helped by swimming. But because of the trigger of cold, he hadn't ever been into the chilly waters of Australia's southerly seas, even in high summer. Here on Wallaby Island, it was different. The water was softly cool, and safely flat. The tiny waves lapped the sand...and Josh's toes...like bits of lace.

He jumped over each one. Nick took his hand and they jumped together, wading out a little further each time, taking it slowly, until Josh was in chest-deep, which Nick decided was far enough. Josh was thrilled about it, leaping and splashing, laughing helplessly when Nick threw him into the air and swung him around, making an arc of wake with Josh's feet.

He's forgotten to be scared of me...

For the moment, at least.

His body was too thin and pale, though, and even in such balmy water he soon began to look purple around the mouth. His teeth were chattering.

'Time to stop,' Nick said.

He turned towards the shore, and there was

Miranda in dark blue jogging shorts and a white
vest top, coming back from a jog along the sand.
He took a breath to call out to her, *Hey, Miranda,
look at Josh in the water!* But then he swallowed
her name back, knowing it would have come out
too eagerly.

She saw them, though, and waved as she
jogged—had probably recognised them when
she'd first arrived for her run. There were several
other people on the beach now, too. How could
you stay in bed or shut away in a cabin on a
morning like this?

Josh didn't argue about stopping. Despite the
warmth of the water, it had chilled him now.
He'd started to wheeze, but wouldn't let Nick
carry him back to the beach. 'I can go myself.'
They waded to the shore together, with Nick listening to every breath. He wrapped his discarded
T-shirt around Josh, grateful for his own size
because the garment practically qualified as a
blanket on a small five-year-old.

'OK, Joshie?'

Josh nodded.

'Your inhaler's back at the cabin.'

'I'm OK,' he wheezed. He had his fists clenched

and his jaw stuck out, but the gestures came from stubbornness, Nick decided, not panic.

Should he be panicking, though? Josh's asthma gear was a hundred or so metres away. The medical centre was twice that distance. The nearest hospital lay across a gap of tropical ocean. Maybe panicking was the right approach.

There was a helicopter rescue service, Nick reminded himself. He wasn't going to overreact yet.

Miranda reached them. She was wheezing, too, from the exertion on her lungs. She had her hands on her hips and her chest was pumping up and down, strands of damp hair stuck to her forehead, ponytail in place, tips of her elfin ears showing, long tomboy legs bare and brown and softly muscled, and that indefinable sense of achievement and satisfaction that Nick always got, too, when he ran, despite the aching legs and fighting lungs.

A surge of sudden and very male desire flooded through him, and he wondered what it would feel like to hold her hot, breathless body in his arms, and how her skin would smell after she'd run on a beach at dawn.

'You look happy,' he said stupidly.

She grinned. 'I love the beach, and I love to run.' Then she added, 'Got your inhaler, Josh?' She'd heard the sound of his breathing.

'Do you want to borrow it?'

'No, sweetheart, I meant for you.'

'I'm OK. It's in the cabin.'

Still breathing hard, Miranda looked at Nick, and he read her easily. 'We'll go back,' he mouthed.

'No drama,' she mouthed back, 'but, yes, I think you should.' Then she turned away and began her cool-down routine of slow stretches, closing her eyes and facing the morning sun.

Nick went to pick Josh up but he shook his head and started off on his own, in a gesture of independence Nick suspected he wasn't allowed to follow through on very often. He followed his son, watching the neat, resolute feet moving rhythmically on the sand, watching him warm up fast in the morning sun, with the damp T-shirt still wrapped around him.

Neither of them spoke, but the silence between them felt fine after their noisy time together in the water. To an outsider, they would have looked as if they were going back to get dressed for breakfast, not in search of lifesaving medication.

Josh was still wheezing by the time the two of them were sitting on his bed with the inhaler and spacer ready. As far as Nick could tell, however, the wheezing hadn't progressed to the frightening tight and struggling stage it often reached.

'Ready for this?' he asked Josh, who nodded, and they managed the dose together with good smooth timing. He breathed more easily at once.

Nick did, too. 'Time for breakfast soon,' he said.

There came a light knock at the cabin door some minutes later, after they'd dressed in dry clothes and were ready to go and eat. Miranda stood there. She'd showered and changed after her run. Nick could smell the lingering scent of shampoo on her damp hair, which lay loose around her shoulders, and she was wearing a skirt and top that looked tropical but sufficiently professional to remind him she wasn't here for a break.

'Everything fine?' she asked.

He knew she was speaking as Josh's doctor, and responded accordingly. 'Yes, the inhaler worked fast today.'

'It wasn't a bad attack. You did the right thing, taking it calmly and letting him walk back on his own.'

'Are you heading over for breakfast?'

'Yes, I'm on my way. Coming, too?'

It seemed logical to walk together, and to sit together once they reached the camp's large communal dining room. Nick remembered how their conversation had limped to a halt last night when he'd refused to continue what he'd begun to say on the beach. He wanted to talk to her, but not about the tough, confronting things. Why put either of them through that? And why avoid her, when there were plenty of easy subjects they could talk about?

'How often do you run?' he asked instead.

'Oh, you know, the usual kind of schedule for that kind of thing.' She grinned, warm eyes alight. 'Every day, except for all the days when I don't.'

He laughed. 'That's about my schedule, too.'

Josh had found Lily. 'Can I take my plate over to the other table?'

'And sit with Lily?'

Josh nodded.

'Of course you can.'

Which left Miranda and Nick not exactly on their own, because there were people all around them and questions she had to answer every few minutes, but there was an odd kind of privacy to their breakfast all the same, and by the time they'd each drunk two cups of coffee and eaten bowls of cereal and yoghurt and fruit, the dining room had almost emptied out and Josh and Lily were chasing each other round the tables.

Nick hadn't even registered how much time must have gone by until Lily fell and scraped her knee, which caught the attention of Charles, who'd been talking to the catering manager over by the kitchen door. He wheeled himself over, and Miranda looked at her watch and gave an exclamation of horror. 'I need to get going!'

So I can still talk to her, Nick thought.

And we can still, both of us, lose all track of time because we're enjoying it so much.

He didn't know what it meant, but he felt a mixture of eagerness and trepidation that was rapidly brewing into a potent cocktail inside him.

How much had he changed? Enough? Or not at all?

CHAPTER FIVE

IT WAS happening. All over again. Miranda was falling for Nick, and falling fast.

Like jumping out of a plane with no parachute.

Like watching a huge wave rolling towards you while you stood waist deep in the ocean, and having no idea whether you should surf, duck or run.

She couldn't run. She was stuck here on the island with him until at least next weekend.

And then he'd leave, and she'd be able to duck the whole problem.

Which would be worse.

OK, no ducking or running. That left…

Surfing.

Oh lord, surfing her feelings for Nick! Did she really mean that? Did she really intend to let herself keep having these lovely relaxed—and only superficially safe—conversations with him? On the beach. In the pottery room. On the glass-bottomed boat that took the whole group on a fabulous reef trip on Monday afternoon.

Was she going to keep looking at him when she had her sunglasses on so that he couldn't see the direction of her gaze? Was she going to keep smiling at him and patting the chair beside her so that he'd come over and sit with her at meals? Or, if he got to the dining room first, keep looking for him because she knew he'd smile and pat the adjacent chair in just the same way?

So he's feeling it, too?

She knew he was. She *thought* he was…

Yes. The looks he gave her. The way he kept losing track of time when they were together. Her heart turned over when he would glance at his watch and get a shocked look on his face. If anything, he'd surrendered to this more than she had, because he was here on a holiday without the professional obligations that kept her just that little bit more cool-headed and in line.

Oh, cool-headed? Who was she kidding? She had a loving heart and she wanted to give it away—the same problem that had haunted her for ten years. She'd given her heart to Nick once before and he'd walked away and that had hurt and scared her so much that she'd never really let Ian make a full claim on her, which hadn't worked either.

So why was she feeling this way? What should she do?

It wasn't as if they'd talked about anything important. She felt totally at a loss to interpret what it all meant. For Nick, this might be nothing more than a holiday fling. Convenient. Fun while it lasted. Something that an experienced man took because it was on offer, without the remotest intention of trying to make it last.

Who says I'm offering?

Her heart felt fickle, one minute beating wildly because he'd walked into view and the next minute hardening itself in a surge of self-protective instinct when she remembered how it felt to be hurt. The on-again, off-again hardened heart was, she thought, the only reason Nick hadn't kissed her yet. Sometimes she gave out a vibe that left him unsure and pushed him just far enough away.

Just.

But maybe I'm looking for a holiday fling, too.

Was she? Was she capable of something like that? Or was she too *nice*?

She thought about it—Monday night, lying in bed unable to sleep despite the busy, sun-filled day, the dawn run on the beach, the soporific sea air. She was thirty-four years old, single, secure. Why not have a fling? They could be scrupulous about protection, set out the ground rules in advance to make sure they were both on the same page. It would add, as some people would tell her, a nuance of delicious spice to her two weeks at Crocodile Creek Kids' Camp and she'd never forget it.

Go for it, Miranda!

Not with Nick.

At one in the morning, and again at three, and then five, this was the point she always reached. Sure, Miranda, have a holiday fling if you want. But don't have it with Nick. Find a sexy hotel waiter, aged twenty-five. The pool boy. The Swedish scuba instructor. Or how about that dyed and corseted lounge singer in the hotel bar last night, strenuously attempting to pass for thirty when he was more like fifty-five?

Yep, even him.

But not Nick.

Nick is too important.

You'll get hurt. Again.

This was what she was left with in the end—a huge, clanging, discordant warning bell in her head telling her over and over the news she didn't want to hear but knew she had to listen to, 'You'll get hurt.'

The sun packed a punch this far north. Miranda felt the sharp heat on her bare shoulders and knew she should put on more sunscreen. At three o'clock on Tuesday afternoon, the shadows from the greenery at the top of the beach had begun to lengthen a little, but she would still begin to burn at any moment.

Most of the kids were in the water. They'd had a morning of crafts, music and games, followed by a siesta after lunch. Miranda had taken one of her asthma patients to the medical centre in the wake of a severe attack triggered by too much running and laughing.

'If she has to have an attack, running and laughing is the best trigger I can think of,' her very sensible mother Julia had said, once her initial fears about her daughter had subsided. 'I should have thought to use her inhaler before-hand, but I didn't think they'd get so active right after lunch. I wonder, though...' She frowned suddenly. 'She's usually more sensible because she hates having a bad attack. She'll come up to me and take some puffs and wait until she feels safe to run around.'

Miranda had noted nine-year-old Kathryn's state of agitation and use of accessory muscles in her struggle to breathe and had decided not to take any risks. She'd helped Beth Stuart to get Kathryn stabilised with oxygen and medication and they'd agreed that Kathryn should stay on corticosteroids for three days and spend the night in the medical centre, before hopefully being cleared for discharge in the morning.

In hindsight, though, she understood Julia Rabey's concern. The nine-year-old had settled into her bed in the medical centre almost too willingly. Was there some attention-seeking going on? She asked Julia an open-ended question about it—any problems at home?—but there didn't seem to be. If Mrs Rabey was hiding something, she was good at it.

There was a lovely, bubbly nurse from the mainland hospital working at the clinic today, Grace Blake, who'd told Miranda, 'My hubby and I are coming to the bonfire and barbecue tonight. His name's Harry. You'll know him if you see him—lovely big Aussie bloke. He's our local cop. The bonfire is a Crocodile Creek Hospital tradition, and we didn't want to be left out just because Charles—that's Dr Wetherby, our director—has temporarily transferred it out to the island. I'll probably see you there.'

'Better there than here in the medical centre.'

'True, and you probably have a couple of patients who can't go because of the smoke.'

But which ones?

Miranda uncapped her sunscreen bottle and ran through the names on her mental list.

Lauren didn't want to go. A beach barbecue? Lame! She and her parents were going for a gourmet dinner at the hotel's five-star restaurant instead. There were several who were keen and should be fine. And there were a few more of her lot who would have their barbecue delivered to the dining room, as would a couple of Benita's patients. The camp catering staff had promised to make it a special occasion with music and games so that the kids wouldn't feel as if they were missing out.

And what about Josh?

Nick appeared beside her at that moment.

Well, not so much *beside* as *over*. He'd just come out of the water and still had a towel slung around his neck while he used the ends to wipe the salt water from his face as he stood just in front of her.

Josh had dropped to the sand nearby and had already begun to play with some of the other kids. With his little body covered in board shorts and a rash vest, he looked like a miniature, dark-haired version of Surfer Jamie, who was showing off his board-paddling techniques to any teenage girls who might be watching, twenty metres from shore. Garf, the golden labradoodle, was on the beach, too, bounding around and chasing a red rubber ball.

Nick spread out his towel and sat down beside Miranda, his knees thrust into the crooks of his elbows as he wrapped his arms across his lower legs. 'I'm wondering about this bonfire and barbecue tonight,' he said, throwing her a brief glance before staring at the water. Behind his sunglasses, Miranda couldn't have seen his eyes even if he'd been looking directly at her. 'Had you thought about whether Josh should go?'

'About five seconds before you sat down. But I hadn't made a decision.'

'He wants to.' Nick controlled a sigh.

'I can understand why you're not sure.'

'Anna would play it super-safe.'

'Do you want to talk to her about it? I'm assuming you're in touch by phone.'

'Morning and evening. I'd actually expected she'd phone more often than that.'

'How is her mother doing?'

'Getting there. They've set the fracture but she's still in hospital. Anna's still negotiating with her sisters about them coming down. I don't want to ask her opinion on the beach bonfire, I just want him to be there. I'm in a rebellious mood, or something. He's having such a great time here. And so am I.'

'Is he nagging you about it?'

'I wish! No, just one tentative little question over breakfast. Am I going, Dad? But every time the subject comes up, I can see his ears pricking and his agitation rising.'

'Smoke is a very obvious trigger for most asthmatics,' Miranda said slowly. She had the open plastic bottle of sunscreen still in her hand, but Nick's question had distracted her from the task of putting it on. Now she felt another prickle of burning on her shoulders and poured some of the white cream into her palm. It was warm and runny from the sun's heat shining on her beach bag.

'If there's a steady breeze, I can keep him away from the smoke,' Nick said. 'But if the air is still, or the wind keeps changing direction, it'd be tougher.'

'In any case, you'd have to be pretty careful.'

'I would. As careful as I possibly could be without cramping Josh's style. Hell, I'm not sure if the kid even has a style, with the way—' He stopped, and Miranda could guess what he'd been about to say.

With the way he spent so much time wrapped in cotton wool.

'He has a style, Nick,' she said. 'Believe it or not, I've actually seen him being quite naughty in hospital a couple of times.'

'Yeah?' He grinned, pleased. 'Like…how naughty?'

'Well, he had several other kids collapsing in

giggles both times, but we didn't need to file an incident report or press criminal charges or anything.'

'That's…that's really good to know, actually.' He gave another grin.

Miranda looked at him, letting her understanding and all the resurgent attraction she'd begun to feel show way too clearly in her face, despite her best intentions. Where was her resolve? Totally elbowed aside by her wilful heart, that was where. Holding back went so much against her nature.

In a moment of insight she saw that she and Ian could never have made a success of their relationship, even if he'd asked her to go to New Zealand with him, when his career had taken him there three years into their relationship, and even if she'd said yes. She'd been chiding herself lately about holding back from him in order to protect herself, but in reality she hadn't loved him with real depth—not the depth she was capable of.

That was why it hadn't worked. That was the only reason it had even been possible for her to hold back in the first place. If she'd really loved

him, holding back would have been un-
thinkable, she'd have been dragged helplessly
onward by her heart.

Where did that leave her now?

Nick's body had dried after his swim, leaving
a residue of fine salt against his darkening
holiday tan. He was sitting too close, and he was
just plain gorgeous. She didn't want to be within
reach of his body, within sight of the silky hairs
on his forearms and the salt on his lips.

Lazily he asked her, 'Want some help with
that?' He gestured at the cream Miranda had just
smeared on her shoulder. It was awkward trying
to reach around and hard to know if she was
covering all the right places, so she'd given up
for the moment, while Nick was talking to her.

'Um, OK,' she said, wondering about the implications of a woman letting a man put sunscreen on her naked back.

And about the implications of a man asking to.

But they were both more concerned, right now,
with the issue of Josh and the bonfire night.

Nick moved to sit behind her. 'I think what I
want,' he said slowly, as his hand made creamy
circles on her skin, 'is your permission as Josh's

doctor for me to at least bring him down here tonight, rather than exiling ourselves to the dining room without even trying. And if you have the slightest doubt about the wind direction or the intensity of the smoke or the way I'm handling it, anything, I want you to tell me very bluntly to take him away.'

'You're a doctor yourself, Nick.'

'I'm a bloody father first!'

The heel of his hand pushed against her spine in unconscious emphasis. He took the sunscreen bottle from her as if he almost hadn't noticed he was doing it, and Miranda heard a squelching sound as he squirted more cream into his hand.

'I don't trust my own instincts with Josh's asthma.'

'You should, Nick. So far this week you've done everything right.'

'Even this thing about the bonfire?' He rubbed the sunscreen into her shoulders and down the backs of her arms.

She could smell the beachy fragrance of it, taking her back through a lifetime of holidays by the water, with her parents sitting sedately beneath umbrellas on folding chairs and Miranda herself soon finding a group of other kids to join in with. She remembered how wistfully she'd wished for the ready-made playmates that siblings had in each other. Josh seemed to be reacting the same way this week.

'You haven't given him an answer yet,' she told Nick. 'You've shared your concerns with me, as his doctor, which was the right first step.'

'Not just as a doctor,' he said. His hands stopped moving but didn't leave her skin. His touch on her shoulders was cooler than the sun and heavy with meaning. 'More than that. As someone I trust and want to get to—'

She half turned. 'Don't.'

'You're not even going to let me finish?'

'You're...you're confusing me with this.'

His voice dropped lower. 'I thought I was getting increasingly clear.'

'I mean it, Nick, just don't. I don't want it. I can't handle it.'

She played with those kids on the beach like their brand-new sister, but then it came time to leave and they went off in a big family group, still laughing and talking, while she was alone with Mum and Dad...

Nick took his hands away, pushed his sunglasses up into his hair and they looked at each other. As he didn't speak, she made the classic mistake of jumping in to fill the gap, her heart right out there on view.

Not particularly nice about it either.

'You never phoned. We had the most wonderful night of my life. We discovered that we knew each other so well. Or that's what I thought. I told you I loved you! And I wasn't the only one who said those words. I really thought you meant them. I walked on air for about twenty-four hours before the first doubt kicked in. I really thought you'd be bursting to pick up the phone. And then you just never did. I even—why am I telling you this?—asked around, in case you'd had some crisis. I was all ready to rush to your hospital bedside, or hop on a plane, or something.'

'Miranda—'

'But, no, you were still in town. You'd taken a job in a restaurant while we waited for our results. And it's ten years later, but you're putting sunscreen on my back and telling me I'm not just your son's doctor, and the fact that you never phoned does actually still *matter*, if you're going to start saying things like that, and doing things like that.'

'I'm not good at talking about this stuff.' It came out as a growl. 'The sunscreen's clear enough, isn't it?' His gaze flicked to her mouth and the look almost felt like a kiss.

'The sunscreen is very, very superficial. And wouldn't I be a fool to trust someone who once hurt me so much?'

She never learned her lesson about the kids on the beach. Day after day, she found friends to play with—sometimes the same ones, sometimes a new group—and every time they said a cheery goodbye—*Maybe we'll see you tomorrow*—and forgot about her as soon as they went home.

'You wanted me to phone? Even after everything I'd said?'

'*Because* of everything you'd said! What had you said? Something terrible? No! You'd shown me your heart!' Far too late, she tried to make light of it. 'Don't you know what that does to a woman?'

'I thought you'd run a mile.'

'Because you showed that you were human?'

'Human is often a euphemism for weak, in my experience,' he drawled.

She lowered her voice. Even humour seemed like too much of a game. 'That's not what I saw in you that night, Nick. It's what I saw in myself, though, after you didn't phone. I lost sleep over it for months, if you want the truth. It took me eighteen months to find someone new, and then that didn't work either, even though we were together for six years.'

'And now?'

'Now? In Melbourne? No one.' In the two and a half years since she and Ian had broken up, she'd been out with a few men, a few times, but nothing had gone very far.

'Good.'

'Irrelevant! Nick, if I have a holiday fling over these next two weeks, I'm sorry, but it's not going to be with you.' She sounded more emphatic about it than she felt.

He flinched. 'That's telling it straight, I guess.'

'You'd prefer mixed signals?'

'No, but the *not with you* part is conjuring up some pictures I don't want to think about.'

She closed her eyes, because she didn't want to see his face. 'I think that's your problem, not mine,' she said, and was pretty sure that she was lying.

Silence.

Opening her eyes, she discovered he was looking at Josh, who'd left the other kids and was coming over to speak to his dad. His breathing had been nice and clear since yesterday morning, and his way of relating to his father was growing perceptibly more comfortable and natural. He even smiled as he said, 'Come and see my castle, Dad.'

She and Nick should both be feeling great, Miranda thought, and yet they weren't. There was an awkwardness now, a sense of disappointment in the air as real as the smell of the sunscreen.

'I need to cool off,' she said, and stood up ready to go into the water.

They avoided each other for the rest of the afternoon. Miranda made an informal round of her patients, listened to several chests and tweaked some medication. She ate the barbecue dinner with the group in the dining room to swell their numbers because, despite the catering staff's best efforts, the kids knew that the beach bonfire was where the action would be tonight.

They were just finishing their meal when Nick appeared in the open doorway and came straight up to Miranda. 'Look, I think these kids could come down,' he said. 'The fire is just a big heap of glowing coals now. It's died right down, and there's no smoke. Josh's chest sounds perfectly clear. I really can't see that they'd have any problems. And we're going to toast marshmallows for dipping in chocolate sauce.'

'We'll try it, then,' Miranda agreed.

A couple of the younger kids and their parents chose to go back to their cabins, because one or two heads were practically falling onto the table with fatigue, but the rest of the dining-room group were eager to join the party.

It was a fantastic sight as they reached the beach. Night had fallen with its usual tropical speed and the pit of coals glowed in the middle of the sand. Miranda could still smell sausages and onions. An older man who seemed to be called Grubby was loading an electric beach buggy with barbecue equipment and coolers of leftovers, while someone else crouched over a wire rack set on the edge of the coals, stirring the chocolate sauce in a thick pot. Its rich aroma soon drowned out the more down-to-earth barbecue smells.

'Charles has turned this into a major event,' said Susie, coming up to Miranda. She was officially off duty and looked relaxed in cool tropical colours that set off her blonde hair. 'I'm sure there are people here that you don't know…'

'There's hardly anyone I do know!'

'I'll run through a few of them.' Susie began a dizzying series of potted biographies and introductions on the hop. 'That's Grace Blake. Oh, right, you do know her, from the medical centre. That's her husband Harry, our local arm of the law, helping Grubby load the barbecue grill. This is Emily and her husband Mike, they're with the hospital on the mainland.'

'Hi, Emily, hi, Mike.'

'And Gina and Cal, too, over there, both doctors, recently married, and that's their little boy, CJ, playing with Josh. Gina's our heart specialist and we're very lucky to have her. There was a bit of a blip in their past, which brought CJ into the picture well before they worked out what they wanted with each other. Oh, and Luke Bresciano and Janey Stafford. Janey blew in with the cyclone and never left. People seem to do that kind of thing around here. Me, I'm supposed to be having a night off and doing my grocery shopping at home on the mainland, but Beth has—' She broke off. 'You know Beth.'

'Dr Stuart. From the medical centre.'

'Of course you know Beth. She offered me her spare bed in the cabin for tonight, and this sounded like much more fun.'

Someone grabbed Susie's attention at that moment, leaving Miranda trying to fix at least a couple of those Crocodile Creek names and relationships in her head. Which one was Janey again? Which one was Cal? She soon gave up on keeping everyone straight.

She saw Nick keeping a close eye on Josh, chocolate sauce getting dripped on the sand from the squishy caramelised marshmallows, Stella actually laughing as she put a marshmallow into her mouth, and one of Benita's cancer kids being carried sleepily off to bed. Lauren arrived with her parents from their five-star-hotel meal. She watched the scene from her wheelchair, her expression disdainful...then she turned to her parents and asked if she could join in.

Not quite clear about her own role, Miranda hung back a little.

Don't get too close to the kids on the beach, because they'll soon be gone, no matter how much you want to play…

Watching Nick again, and remembering what he'd said about talking—that he wasn't good at it—she wondered if the two of them had more issues in that area than she'd realised. Odd, contradictory things in common. Not knowing how much it was safe to give. Holding back at the wrong times. They both had uneasy relationships with their own passionate hearts.

She and Ian had met through medicine. They'd always struggled for time together due to their long hours of specialised training, and had spent the final three years of their six-year relationship an ocean apart.

Not a huge ocean, just the Tasman Sea because he'd gone to work in New Zealand on what was supposed to be a one-year appointment. But it had been extended, then extended again. Miranda had flown across whenever she could, or Ian had flown to Melbourne, but when he'd finally announced that he'd accepted the position in Christchurch on a permanent basis…

She'd waited for him to ask her to come with him, because she'd had a rule with Ian all along. Don't be the first one to give. Don't be the first one to say *I love you*. Play the cards-to-your-chest game, because you can get hurt if you don't.

He hadn't asked.

'So…' he'd said instead, vaguely, and they'd looked at each other and just known without question that it was over. A few more minutes of conversation had sealed the fact.

Why am I thinking about Ian so much this week?

Because she couldn't help watching Nick, even though she knew she shouldn't. To him, she'd given her whole heart without question, and maybe she'd never really managed to grab all of it back again…

The frisbee game was in full swing. Harry and Grubby shooed everyone away from the dying coals and shovelled sand over the fire, ending up with a big, warm heap that they warned wouldn't be safe to go near for hours yet. 'The tide'll come in, cool it down and wash it away.'

Charles sat in his wheelchair with a mobile

phone pressed to his ear, struggling to keep out the beach noise so he could manage a conversation. 'I wouldn't be a very good one,' Miranda heard him say, although so far the impression she had from people like Beth and Susie was that, despite the wheelchair, he was good at almost everything.

His phone call seemed to launch a whole concert of mobile phone ringtones. The island had good coverage from a couple of discreetly placed towers. Stella had received a text message. Lauren was talking into her phone. 'There's no one cool. Well, maybe one guy...' Susie grabbed hers from her pocket as it began to ring, and when she heard the voice at the other end, her face lit up and she went off into the darkness with a hand pressed over her free ear to shut out the noise from the beach.

But when Miranda went to check on Kathryn Rabey in the medical centre a few minutes later, she found Susie huddled on a bench at the side of the path, in tears which she at once realised she couldn't hide.

She dredged up a wobbly smile and waved her on instead. 'Don't mind me, Miranda. I'm fine. I'm being very silly.'

'You don't look fine.'

'How tactful of you to point that out.'

'Sorry. I'm going. I am. Just thought you might want to talk.'

Once again, was this a case of not knowing when to walk away from the kids playing on the beach? They got on well, she and Susie, but as a friendship, it was very new and very temporary.

Playing it safe, she began to walk on, but then Susie said, 'Maybe I should. If *you* think I'm awful, I can deal with it! So-o-o much easier to talk to near-strangers sometimes than to sisters and best friends!' She clapped her fingers against her mouth. 'Oh, the near-stranger thing sounded rude, didn't it? See, I'm a catty witch.'

'No,' said Miranda. 'You're just upset.'

'No, I'm a catty witch. Sit!' Susie patted the seat beside her, the way Nick had been patting the seat beside him in the dining room at each meal.

Miranda sat, then said, 'So tell me. The phone call wasn't announcing that you'd won the lottery, I'm guessing.'

'My sister's pregnant. I told her I was thrilled. And I am. But…'

'Ah…yeah, OK.' Miranda sighed.

'You don't understand.'

'You think?' She made a tick-tock sound with her tongue. 'I'm single, female, childless and thirty-four.'

Susie laughed, eyelashes still wet. 'Well, hon, you got it in one. Not just the clock, though.'

'No?'

'We're twins, you see. Identical. We look spookily alike, and we're supposed to spookily buy the same outfits as each other without knowing, and spookily fall in love with spookily similar men and spookily give birth on the same day. At this rate, it's not even going to happen in the same decade.'

'And you want it. Needless to say.'

'I've always wanted it.' She blinked. 'Hannah didn't, for a long time. She picked the big medical career, I went for the one where you can easily work part time so you can stay home with your family. Now she has the career, *and* the man, *and* she's having the baby, and I hate it that I'm jealous of my own twin, and I hate it that she's having such a huge, life-changing experience that I don't know anything about and can't share and don't look like ever sharing, the rate things are going, when we've shared so much all our lives. But I don't have a man. Even though I'm not a personality-challenged hag, Miranda.'

'Not that I've noticed so far…'

'I'm…I'm *nice*, and funny, sometimes, and I'm halfway pretty. Seven out of ten.'

'Might even give you an eight.'

'Eight! Not bad! And I take care of my body, and I don't have any secret vices, and none of my past boyfriends have put out restraining orders against me for slashing the tyres on their sports cars—'

'Well, there's your problem, right there,' Miranda said.

'What?'

'Going out with men who drive sports cars.'

'Are you trying to make me laugh so I'll stop crying and shut up?'

'It's a good strategy. Don't knock it. I'm hoping someone'll do the same for me next time I go into the biological clock rant.'

'Oh, you've done the biological clock rant, too?'

'What do you think? It's hard! I bet your sister says the same things to you that my non-single-

and-childless friends say to me. All that rubbish about *when the time is right* and *don't try too hard* and *when you least expect it.*'

'Doesn't it make you want to scream?'

'But then I remember they're saying it because they care.'

'Which Hannah is, too, and Emily, my friend here, who married Mike in the middle of the cyclone seven months ago.' Susie sat up straight suddenly. 'I bet Emily's pregnant, too! I just bet she is! Grr! She's been *looking* pregnant lately. She's been a bit weird, all round. Of course! Because she's scared to tell me!'

Miranda gave a sympathetic groan. 'And it's worse when they don't tell you, isn't it, because then you know they've been trying to spare your feelings. They're being kind.'

'At least Hannah didn't do that. She had the testing kit still in one hand and the phone in the other, and I could hear Ryan in the background, begging her to sit down and put her feet up. He is going to be *revolting* for the next seven and a half months, I am so glad they're in New Zealand!' She sniffed, wiped her eyes with the heel of her hand and laughed at herself. 'Gee, that's starting to feel good. I'm not really glad they're in New Zealand. Meanwhile, who else can I unjustly slam?'

'We'll start a list. Can I add names of my own?'

'No, but you can tell me how come you're childless and single and thirty-something, if you want, so that we're even.'

'You really want the total heart-to-heart package tonight, don't you?'

'Only if you want.'

'It might help.'

And Susie put on such a good listening face that Miranda gave in and told it all, stopping short of Nick's name.

Just.

She finished after a few minutes, 'It never occurred to me, you see, that it wasn't safe to give my heart to someone who seemed to want it so much. But when it turned out that way—when he wasn't interested—well…The next time I don't think I gave my heart enough. Once bitten, twice shy. Only that didn't work out either. So now I'm stuck, and I don't know which way to go.'

'Give it,' Susie said promptly.

'Just like that?'

'You can't live life without taking risks. And, anyway, to be brutally honest, when it comes to this kind of thing I don't see that any of us has a choice.'

'Oh, lord, am I ready for that kind of wisdom, I wonder?'

'Clearly we need to go into a relationship counselling practice together, hon.'

They laughed again, a satisfying peal, which cut off abruptly when Nick strode into view along the path. 'Miranda, is that you?'

'Yes, it is.' She stood up at once, thinking of Josh. Nick was frowning and walking too fast. That evening's theme accessory, a mobile phone, was pressed to his ear. 'Is everything OK?'

'Anna wants to speak to you,' he answered shortly. 'I couldn't find you on the beach.' He glanced at Susie, as if something about their shared laughter made him suspicious and unhappy. 'I've found her, she's here,' he said into the phone, then held it out.

'Miranda?' Anna said on the line.

'Hi, Anna.' The other woman's voice came as

a shock. She'd hardly thought about Nick's ex-wife since they'd arrived.

'Please, tell me he doesn't really have Josh at a bonfire!'

'They've buried it in sand now. They handled it really well, Anna, honestly. They lit it early and didn't let any of the asthma or CF kids near it until the flames and smoke had died back to coals. No one has had breathing problems. It's been such a nice night, and Josh had a ball. Even Ming Tan went down there for about half an hour and didn't need her inhaler.'

'Is he eating properly? Or is it just junk?'

'He's eating fine,' Miranda soothed her again. 'You know they wouldn't have a junky menu plan at a place like this. How is your mother doing, by the way?'

'Oh, better. She actually sent me out shopping today.'

'What did you buy?'

'A new swimsuit, shoes…and I had lunch all on my own in the corner of a café, reading a book. I can't remember how long it is since I've done something like that.' She sounded a little bemused at the fact that she'd had some breathing space and had actually enjoyed it. Miranda suspected it might be the healthiest thing that had happened to her in a while. But Anna wasn't to be distracted for long. 'Why is Nick keeping Josh up so late? Can you please stress to him—?'

'Because there are fun things to do in the evenings,' Miranda cut in, firm and cheerful. 'So it's the best plan. It's pretty hot during the day. Most kids have a siesta or at least some quiet time after lunch.'

'Miranda, you know the background to my son's situation.'

'I'm keeping that in mind, Anna. And I can only say, from everything I've seen, he's having a really fabulous time, and so is his dad.'

Thick silence.

Miranda had the sudden shocked understanding that a part of Anna—the deep, murky and all too human part where an identical twin could be jealous of her beloved sister's pregnancy, or a well-adjusted professional woman could covertly roll her eyes and wish her best friend would just *shut up* about the right man coming along when you least expected it—yep, that same part of Anna didn't *want* Josh to have a good time.

Not when he was having it with Nick.

With an urgency that surprised her, Miranda turned her back on Susie and Nick, still standing nearby, and went further down the path.

'Anna, you have to rethink what you're feeling,' she said. 'You have to look at some of your reactions, sit them side by side with your love for Josh and see what's happening here.'

'What do you mean by that?'

'Josh is having a great time. That's what matters. It's all that matters. His breathing sounds great. He looks happy. He's eating well. Whether he's with Nick or with you, his happiness is what's important.' She waited a moment for Anna's agreement, then added insistently, 'Isn't it?'

'Of course.' A little wooden and uncomfortable.

'And I'm not just speaking as your son's doctor, I'm speaking as someone who wants the best for all three of you. If you're jealous of the time Nick's getting to spend with him this week—'

'*Jealous?*'

'That's a very human response, in a lot of ways, but you're the one who's getting twisted up inside over it, Anna. You have to see that, and let it go. Take more of those café lunches. Remember that you're a person, too.'

'W-why are you saying this?' Anna stammered. She sounded indignant and yet unsure of herself, too. 'I mean, how dare you say it? I have never asked for this sort of personal interference from you, Dr Carlisle, and I don't want it.'

'Anna, don't you think—?'

'No. No. There's nothing more to say. Good grief, I can't believe this! Over the phone!'

'All right, I'm sorry if I was too frank. I know you didn't ask for it, but I believe it needed to be said. Don't use Josh as a weapon in your battles with Nick. And don't forget about your own needs as a human being. Step back. Do what's best for your son, and for yourself. Right now, I don't think you are. You're dying inside—your needs, your capacity for joy—and it's not helping your child.'

'You are really not pulling your punches tonight!'

'Not this time, no.'

Another silence, then Anna said stiffly, 'I'll think about what you've said.'

Miranda spoke more gently this time. 'I know you will, Anna.'

But she was almost shaking when she flipped the phone shut a moment later. She'd never spoken so passionately and frankly to the mother of a patient before, especially not a patient she cared about the way she cared about little Josh. Was she wrong to have stuck her neck out so far? Had she stepped over the wrong line?

And, above all, what would Nick think?

Nick, about whom Susie had just unknowingly told her that she didn't have a choice.

He couldn't have heard, but he must have realised from her tone and her determined retreat that she was saying something important. He was chatting with Susie when she reached them again. It was a little tense and superficial on both sides. Susie's face still showed traces of her recent tears, and Nick wasn't exactly in a relaxed frame of mind either.

Miranda told him, 'I think we've sorted it out.'

'Is she coming up?'

'Oh. We didn't cover that. Has one of her sisters come down from Sydney?'

'I mean coming up to take Josh home straight

away. She talked about it.' He glanced at Susie, apparently decided he didn't care that she was listening, and added, 'Well, threatened it. Because I let him go down to the bonfire.'

'I'm sure she won't.' Despite Anna's difficult nature, Miranda had underlying faith in her. She was emotional and irrational, and having an only child with serious health issues had narrowed her perspective to a dangerous degree, but she wasn't stupid. At some point, surely, she'd start to see things more clearly and be more willing to let go. 'She'll rethink things.'

'Hmm,' Nick said. He took some restless paces on the sandy path. He seemed shut away suddenly, and Miranda didn't know what more she could tell him.

Susie touched her shoulder and said, 'I'm going back to the beach, Miranda. See if there's anything I can help with. They'll be winding up soon.'

'Where's Josh?' Miranda asked Nick, when Susie had gone. He was still standing there with the mobile phone held forgotten in his hand. At her words, he thrust it into his pocket and shifted his mental focus.

'Still playing,' he said. 'One of the Crocodile

Creek doctors said she'd keep an eye on him. Janey someone. She has her son here, too, and they're about the same age. But I should get him home to bed.'

He was silent for a moment, but Miranda could see that he hadn't finished. Even in the dim light she could see the lines of tension around his eyes and mouth. She wanted to touch his face with her fingers and soothe them away. Oh, Susie was right! What choice did she have, where he was concerned?

Finally, he spoke again. 'What did you and Anna say to each other? Can I ask?'

'You'd better not.' She blurted out, 'I'm already in danger of getting too involved. No, to be honest, I already *am* too involved.'

He stepped closer and said softly, 'As a doctor or as a woman?' He was looking at her intently now, examining her face in a way that made her whole body heat up. His eyes glinted darkly. His hand hovered ready to touch her and yet he didn't do it. He was waiting for her answer, but she couldn't give it. 'Miranda? This isn't what you said today on the beach.'

'I know.'

'So tell me. I want to hear it, not guess at it.'

She closed her eyes. 'Both. As a doctor, and as a woman. It's obvious, isn't it? Both!'

And then she just stood there and waited, because she knew down to the marrow of her bones that he was going to kiss her.

CHAPTER SIX

SHE remembered this. The way he tasted. The way his mouth moved. The strength of his body against hers. The intensity of his focus.

Before Miranda could think about the impossible contradiction in having turned Nick away this afternoon only to kiss him with her whole soul now—she'd never stopped seeking out the kids on the beach, after all, and at heart she was proud of her child-self for that—she had parted her lips and wrapped her arms around him. She couldn't speak or think. She could only feel.

Feel, and remember.

This was exactly how it had been ten years ago. One minute acting like strangers, the next minute knowing that life hadn't properly begun until now, until this moment, when she was touching him. It was like a door being flung open to show a fabulous mountain vista instead

of a tame suburban yard, or a word puzzle re-
solving from a meaningless jumble of letters
into a classic phrase.

This was right.

She belonged in this moment.

'Miranda…' he whispered.

She'd never been kissed so deeply. Where did
his mouth end and hers begin? She hardly knew.
He tasted of marshmallow and chocolate, and
his skin smelled like seawater and sunscreen, as
fresh and inviting as the ocean itself. He sought
her response with a silent mixture of command
and entreaty that frayed her control so fast she
was breathless. He couldn't get enough of her,
and she felt the same. Every touch of their hands
on each other's bodies staked a demanding claim.

It was serious, this kiss.

It wasn't opportunistic or semi-drunk or half-
hearted or merely physical.

It asked questions and made promises and
changed everything. It was built on everything
that had happened ten years ago, but this only
made it more inevitable, not more impossible.
She knew it, and he knew it, and neither of them
wanted it to stop.

But Josh was still on the beach, and Nick couldn't leave him in a stranger's care for much longer, even if the stranger was a local medical centre doctor with a child of her own.

'Could you come and sit on my veranda when Josh is asleep?' he whispered, his arms so warm and solid around her that she thought she'd feel safe in them forever.

'I—Yes. Um, yes, I will. If you want.'

'Of course I want! Watching you talk to Anna on the phone just now, with so much heat and urgency in your voice even when I couldn't hear the words, hearing you laugh with Susie like old friends when you've only known each other for two days…Talk to *me*! Laugh with *me*. Put that heat into your voice when you talk to *me*!' He gave a metallic laugh and admitted, 'I was jealous.'

'Jealous? Were you?' Something nagged and fluttered in the back of her mind as she spoke, but she didn't have time to examine it now. Something to do with the words he'd just spoken.

'Yes, because I remembered that we'd talked and laughed like that once, too,' he was saying.

'We did,' she said on a shaky breath. 'Suddenly it feels like yesterday.'

'Come back to the beach with me. Come to the cabin and wait while I get Joshie to bed. We're not letting this go.'

'No, we're not...'

He took her hand and they stumbled down the sandy path, disorientated by the power of what had just happened.

On the beach, the bonfire party was almost over. Kids were yawning and parents, camp staff and medical people were looking at their watches or packing up gear. It was nearly nine o'clock, and any of the Crocodile Creek people who needed to be back on the mainland tonight would have to leave very soon in order to make the last boat at nine-fifteen.

'Come on, Rowdy!' Janey said to her little boy, echoing similar hurry-up phrases from other parents.

Josh stood ankle deep in the water, apparently mesmerised by the moonlight glowing on the white foam. Nick went down to him and took his hand, and Josh looked up at him in a way that would probably bring Nick's heart close to bursting. Miranda waited, not wanting to interrupt the moment. They'd already made so much progress together.

Charles was still here.

She was surprised to see him on his feet, although he leaned heavily on a sturdy frame and had his wheelchair just behind him. He did have some use of his legs, then. He looked tired, and as if he was fighting the fatigue way too hard, refusing to give in to it until he had no choice. With his disability or without it, he was an incredibly impressive man.

She heard him ask one of the Crocodile Creek doctors... Luke, maybe... 'Where's Lily? She was here just a minute ago. Dammit, I hate it when she runs off in the dark!'

Or rather, he hated his own inability to go easily in search of her, Miranda realised. The beach was soft and treacherous for either wheels or a frame, and he was stuck where he was. He moved back towards his wheelchair and seemed to relax when he saw Lily coming towards him.

She was carrying something. 'I need to show Charles. He'll help.'

The dark shape flopped in her outstretched

hands and Miranda couldn't tell what it was until Lily was just a few metres away. Another child's forgotten piece of clothing?

No, ugh, a dead bird…

'Look! It's sick.'

'It's dead…'

'Can you make it alive?' Lily brought it directly to Charles and held it out with her usual air of confidence and faith in adult power. Miranda didn't know much about birds, but it looked like a migratory seabird. There were a number of such species, she thought, and struggled to come up with some names. Petrels? Terns? Mutton-birds?

'Lily, no…' Charles said, looking down at the creature. He touched it. 'It's still warm. That means it's only just died, but it is dead. Put it down on the sand, Lily.'

'But can't you make it come back alive?'

'I'm a people doctor, Lil, not a bird doctor, and anyway it's dead. I can't bring it back.'

'But I saw it move…'

'You probably did. It must have been its last flutter. It hasn't been dead for long. But it is dead now, I promise, and there's nothing we can do. Luke?' Again, he'd had to turn to a fellow doctor for help, and again he didn't like it.

'Bury it?' Luke suggested. 'I think we'd better. We don't want the kids mucking around with it.' He turned to Janey and their son. 'You should head for the boat. I'll catch up. I'll bury it up in the bushes, where the kids don't dig. Maybe find something to wrap it in.'

'Let me,' Miranda offered. 'There were some paper bread-bags, weren't there?'

'The garbage has all been taken away.'

'I'll find something.'

'Don't worry, we'll just bury it as it is,' Luke said. 'The sand's soft, I can dig a good deep hole very easily.'

'Josh has his plastic shovel,' Miranda realized out loud.

She turned to look. Father and son were still down by the water, unaware of what was happening with Lily's dead bird. Nick had the beach shovel in one hand, along with a red plastic bucket in the other. She loped down to him and asked for the shovel. It was about two feet long, with a nice strong square head.

'What's the problem?' Nick asked.

'Lily has too much faith in Charles's healing powers. I'll explain later. It's no big deal.'

She went back and gave Luke the shovel and he said, 'Thanks. There are some roots, but I should be able to cut through those with this.' He slid the bird onto the shovel. 'Wonder why it died. I can't see any obvious sign of injury. It's thin…'

'Natural causes, then?'

'Yes, it must have been sick…'

The incident of the dead bird cast a shadow over the evening's end. Charles told Lily, 'Go and wash your hands in the water, and then we'll do them properly with soap when we get back to the cabin.'

Lily ran obediently down to the water where she splashed her hands…and most of the rest of her, too, in the process.

Nick and Josh arrived just as Luke finished shovelling sand into the little grave. By now they were almost the last people on the beach. 'Let's get you to bed, kid,' Nick told his son, and Miranda followed them along the path to their cabin.

Josh was asleep within ten minutes…

* * *

Miranda looked lovely and a little nervous, waiting for him on the veranda. Nick could see her through the open window, and when he went to the kitchen to put on the electric jug for tea, he knew he was stalling.

I'm nervous, too.

He wasn't sure why he'd kissed her on the path half an hour ago.

Well, because he'd wanted to, of course, but wanting was never enough, wanting was only the start. There had to be a heck of a lot more, and it had to run so much deeper.

He and Anna had found that out the hard way. It had been such an easy, obvious relationship on the surface. They'd been attracted to each other. They shared certain things—a scrupulous work ethic, an appreciation for some of life's finer offerings.

Anna collected Victorian silver while he collected antique chess sets, and they'd spent some great days browsing garage sales and antiques auctions and flea markets together before Josh's birth. The shared interest had given them something safe and impersonal to talk about, and Anna hadn't seemed to mind that they never truly plumbed each other's emotional depths, never connected on a whole lot of levels.

He'd been relieved about this lack of depth, to the extent that he understood it at the time. The shattering sense of vulnerability and nakedness he'd felt with Miranda had still haunted him when he and Anna had first met, even though at that point it had been more than a year since the night of the fateful medical students' party.

But everything changed with Josh's arrival, almost three years into their marriage.

It was a common enough pattern, Nick knew. Some relationships, like some plants, only thrived in full sunshine and heat. As soon as the first frost fell and life's darker moments hit, the whole thing withered and died. The roots proved to be too shallow. Was that what love meant? Growing deep roots? He didn't think he and Anna had ever loved each other in the right way.

With Josh's birth, she no longer even wanted to find time for antique browsing. The meticulous, hard-working, obsessive part of her personality switched in full from career and hobbies to the baby, and if she hadn't deliberately shut Nick out of her relationship with their son at first, it certainly became deliberate once his asthma developed and their marriage soured so badly.

And with no pattern already in place for talking about their emotions, no way to cut to the heart of what each other thought and felt, he didn't known how to challenge her behaviour until it was too late.

The electric jug boiled and clicked off, and he poured hot water into the mugs. He didn't want a cup of tea and very possibly Miranda didn't want one either, but like the other night he needed a prop, something to hide behind.

She heard him coming, turned from watching the moonlit glimpses of the water and smiled at him.

Nervously.

She was thirty-four, his own age. She understood as well as he did that the best kiss in the world was only the very beginning.

'It seemed easy half an hour ago,' he said, without a second's thought.

Hell! Why did she do this to him? He couldn't hold anything back. Ever. It was as if they picked up effortlessly on a conversation they'd been having their whole lives—a conversation that involved so much more than words.

Everything came spilling out with no censor-ship, no tact, no instinct for self-preservation—all of which he usually had in spades. It was as if, when he was with her, a great big hand came reaching down inside him, rummaging right into his emotions and churning everything to the surface.

With Miranda, what he felt, he said.

Was this why the sight of her had hit him so hard two years ago, when she'd first become Josh's doctor? Was this why he hadn't fought harder against the way Anna excluded him from Josh's health problems?

Pure, naked fear?

She didn't reply. He put the unwanted mugs of tea on the deck railing and watched her stand and come towards him, tentative and stubborn at the same time. Hell, and he felt so tentative himself, with a tingling sense of danger and challenge.

'Just kiss me again,' she said. 'Let's try that.'

'Yeah…?' he whispered, secretly thrilled that she was making the first move, and relieved that she was letting his unintended admission slide.

'Somehow everything seemed to make sense when you did earlier,' she told him softly.

'I'm…kind of testing out whether we get the same effect again.' She tilted her head to one side and gave him a crooked, almost impish smile.

Oh, lord…

He didn't need any further invitation.

First, he touched her shoulders, rediscovering her fine, strong bone structure and the soft skin on either side of her silky top's two thin straps. She looked up at him, her eyes huge and dark and quietly watchful in the cool light.

She didn't fully trust him, yet. He could see it in her face, and it made something twist inside him to watch her taking this step towards his heart while she honestly believed that the ground might easily give way beneath her feet. She was braver than he was…

Oh, hell, and maybe the ground would give way!

He really, really didn't want to hurt her, and yet the enormity of the alternative made his stomach drop with dread.

Could he do it again? Could he strip himself bare? Give everything? Risk so much?

Somehow, he understood that there was no middle road in this case, no safe, shallow-soiled piece of ground the way there had been in his marriage to Anna.

With Miranda, it would be all or nothing. Deep roots, or barren terrain.

And *all* couldn't happen without this terrifying yet desperately wanted first step.

He bent his head, nuzzled his nose against hers, and then his cheek against her cheek. He understood the meaning of his own gestures far too clearly.

The boot's on the other foot, Miranda. I'm the one who's telling you this time, don't hurt me.

He hated this evidence of his Achilles' heel and fought it off, focusing on the one indisputable reality that was coursing through his body.

I want her.

Oh, hell, he wanted her so much!

It surged in him suddenly, with a power that took his breath away, and there was no more nuzzling. He crushed his mouth against hers, dragged the loop of elastic from her ponytail and tangled his fingers in her hair, pulled her against him so that her neat breasts flattened against his chest.

He could feel her nipples, hard through her

barely-there bra. He could feel her breathing, uneven and shallow. He could feel the swelling heat at the apex of her thighs pressing into him, answering the painful, rock-like hardness straining against the front of his baggy beach shorts.

He grabbed her backside, wanting her even closer, and she rocked her hips against him, making him wild with need. He wanted to be inside her, to bring her to the edge and tumbling over it with his touch and his hard length, with the lap of his tongue against the soft inner skin of her lip.

'I'm such a slow learner,' she muttered, on a sound that might have been a sob or a laugh.

'What's wrong?' He could feel a new resistance in her body, but it was ambivalent. She was fighting herself.

'You have a big double bed in there, don't you?' she said. 'And you want me in it, and as soon as you say the word, I'm going to peel off my clothes and go.'

'Yeah...?' He couldn't stop himself from grinning about it like a teenager, his mouth still only a few inches from hers.

She saw the grin and said shakily, 'You are so-o-o missing my point here.'

'You're scared,' he answered. 'I know that.'

'Yes, I'm very scared.'

He took a breath. 'Well, so am I.'

'Of different things.'

'Maybe…No,' he corrected himself, sure of his ground suddenly. 'The same things. I'm scared of exactly the same things.'

'What things, then?' He could feel the whisper of her breath against his upper lip as she spoke.

'Of making ourselves too raw. Of having our trust smashed. Of it just not working out for any one of a hundred reasons, and ending up messy and painful and complicated. I hate regret. It's such a destructive, obsessive feeling. It holds you back, pushes you in totally the wrong direction.'

'What have you regretted, with me?'

'That I said too much. Words can be so dangerous. And then, much later, that I didn't phone you.'

'You regretted that?'

'Of course I did! I carried your phone number around on a piece of paper in my pocket for six months.'

'Then why didn't you use it?'

'Well…Do you know what I did do, in the end?'

'What, Nick?' She pulled away from him, curving her palms round his jaw and pushing lightly, and she laughed at him—perplexed, willing to listen, poised to be angry if she decided it was necessary.

'I burned the piece of paper,' he said.

'There were half a dozen other ways you could have found out my number. Not to mention several easier ways to get rid of it on a piece of paper. Six months, though? You had my phone number in your wallet for six months, before you—? And did you really—?'

'Burn it, yes. Act of self-preservation.' He thought about that for a moment. 'No, actually it was more like taking the easy way out.'

'That doesn't make sense, Nick.'

'I'm not saying any of this makes sense. I know there were other ways I could have got in touch with you. I knew where you lived, I knew several of your friends. Keeping the phone number for so long was…I don't know. A talisman. Burning it was a recognition of my own…' Say it, Nick. He took a breath. 'My own failure.'

She wasn't deflected. If she thought he'd failed, ten years ago, it didn't seem relevant to her now. 'Are you going to take the easy way out tonight?'

'No…'

'Or tomorrow? Tomorrow would be worse. Please, please, don't take the easy way out tomorrow.'

'How many days do you want promises for?' he asked, and felt her body turn rebellious in his arms.

'All right. It's an unreasonable request. This…feels unreasonable, Nick. The demands I want to make are unreasonable.'

'Make them anyway,' he invited her, but she shook her head.

Maybe he didn't need her to say it.

This felt unreasonable to him, too.

Drastically, earth-shatteringly unreasonable and impossible to resist.

'Just kiss me again,' she said. 'Take me to bed.'

The simplicity of it stunned him, in the end.

They left the veranda in silence, hand in hand like schoolchildren.

His room was dark and the tropical air kept it warm even with opened windows. He didn't want to turn on the light. Didn't some people consider it prudish to make love in the dark?

Nick loved it that way, especially in a place like this, so alive, so warm. He loved how the shadows wrapped around the two of them and cocooned them together. Loved the soft, bluish light that did filter into the room from the moonlit world outside.

In it, Miranda's eyes looked even deeper, her mouth even softer, the curves on her smooth-skinned body sculpted by highlights and shadows. She pulled her vest top over her head, unfastened her bra and let it fall, her movements deft and unselfconscious.

Then, with her hands poised at the waistband of her shorts, and her soft breasts cradled by slightly rounded shoulders, she smiled at him. She'd turned impish again, with her head tilted and her eyebrows raised, and he realised it was an invitation— Hey, get your kit off, you! I'm not doing this on my own!

Grinning back at her, he stripped in moments, and found one of the small packets in a side pocket of his suitcase that he'd never removed after the separation because…just because. It wasn't the kind of thing you thought to do. He'd only redis-covered them while packing for this trip.

In darkness, with no blinds over the windows, they were a part of the night. The sounds they made as they began to kiss blended with the wash of the ocean and the rustle of leaves. The breeze blew a faint flavour of salt into the room, and it mingled with the salt still on their skin.

Oh, lord, she was so beautiful!

She felt beautiful, all warm and soft and supple and giving. Her mouth was a peach. Her breasts had cherries on top. He ran his mouth down to her collar-bone and then lower, buried his face between those cherry-tipped breasts, ran his tongue round nipples so sensitive that she was gasping and writhing at the first moment of contact.

She buried her fingers in his hair and clung to him and her responsiveness heightened his own need. They fell to the bed with Miranda on top of him, a lithe featherweight with skin that felt like satin. She poised herself over him and he ran his hands down her body, stopping to cup her backside and slide his fingertips along the creases at the tops of her thighs.

When she let her weight rest against him, he

just wanted to thrust into her right then and there, but he made himself wait, in an agony of restraint, and she kissed his whole body into madness. Lips. Chest. Everywhere.

He groaned out his need and said her name and she slid deliberately all along his length and found his mouth again. 'Problem?' she whispered cheekily.

'No. No problems at all.'

By now, he really couldn't bear to wait and she seemed to know it. She guided him inside her, her hand cuffing him firmly and still that cheeky grin on her face. Then their hips locked together and all he could do was move against her body in a primal rhythm that left no room for words or thoughts, until they cascaded back to earth in showers of sparks.

He felt shaken and breathless and humbled afterwards.

'So, earth move for you, then, did it?' she asked, tender and teasing at the same time. She snuggled against him, wriggling her body like an animal settling in for sleep.

'Boy, you are cheeky!' His voice came out scratchy. 'When did you get this cheeky?'

She didn't answer. Not directly, anyway. 'But it was good, wasn't it?' And only now did he hear the slight note of doubt and questioning in her voice. The cheekiness had been a piece of slick bravado. She honestly hadn't known how good it had been for him.

'Oh-h, yeah!' he said. 'Yes, Miranda. Yes and yes and yes.'

'Oh, that's…nice.'

He liked the fact that sometimes she, too, was lost for the right words.

They lay in silence, contemplating how good it had been, and how good it still was. He had no desire whatsoever to hurry her out of his bed. She could stay here all night…

No, she couldn't.

She was the first to point it out. 'You won't want me here in the morning when Josh wakes up.'

'It's a long time until morning.'

'True.'

They contemplated this, too.

'But what if we both fall asleep?' she said. 'Or he has a nightmare, or an asthma attack, and comes in? Have you ever slept with—?'

He cut her off. 'No, I haven't. If you're going

to ask if I've slept with another woman since the divorce while Josh was under my roof, no. It's only been a year. Less than two years since we separated. I've been out with a couple of women. I haven't brought any of them home.'

'Then we should think about the implications,' she said gently.

They thought about them.

'Don't go yet,' Nick said, because, selfishly, he just didn't want her to.

Later, yes.

In the early hours, after they'd both slept entwined in each other's arms, she'd have to leave.

But not now.

He wanted more of this. The love-making. The talking. The way she snuggled against him. 'The thing is, though, Josh is never under my roof overnight,' he said after a few moments.

The words had drummed in his head, repeating themselves several times before he actually said them out loud. He'd rehearsed them and rejected them, torn between how honest and important they were, how much he wanted to test his courage by talking openly to Miranda and how much he didn't want to ruin the mood.

In the end, he'd chosen honesty because it was
the thing that scared him the most.

'Anna sees to that,' he finished.

'Never? Really never?' She wasn't surprised,
though, he could tell. Having heard Anna's
version of events as Josh's doctor, she must
know that he hadn't been given much time with
his son. 'Have you tried to fight it, Nick?'

'I've done everything except go to court. That
I won't do, for Josh's sake. I do have some faith
in Anna, that she'll eventually let go of him a
little more. She has to. He's still only five. As I
said, it's less than two years since the separation.' He wanted to stress this to her, somehow
needed her to know that he hadn't jumped into
bed with a whole lot of women since, and hadn't
abandoned his son. 'The asthma thing rocked her
so much. She'd never had anything to do with
illness before, and she overreacted.'

'She was already somewhat over-involved
with Josh before his diagnosis, though, wasn't
she? That's the impression I've had.'

'Yes, you're right.' He felt an intense relief that
she'd taken an independent view, that she knew
his ex-wife and his son as a medical profes-

sional. She understood that Anna was seriously over-involved and didn't automatically buy Anna's own message that he didn't care enough.

He needed her to understand, somehow, and the need was familiar. Ten years ago, he'd also wanted her to know everything about what was important in his life. He'd spilled it all, and then he'd run, terrified of the implications. Hell, was he brave enough not to run now?

'I've seen a couple of mothers like that,' she was saying carefully. 'Professional women, accustomed to complete control in their work environment, who think that they can control parenthood in the same way. They disinfect every toy, mash every carrot personally, don't let their crawling babies onto the floor unless there's a clean blanket laid down, go to pieces when the baby won't conform to the routine they've set up so perfectly on paper.'

'Oh, yes, all of that. If her own friends had been having babies at the same time, it might have been different, but at twenty-six she was the first, and she didn't connect with the mothers in her childbirth class. And I was working too hard. I was still finishing my surgical training when he was small. There were too many hours and days and weeks when I wasn't at home, so what right did I have to question what she was doing with our son? None, I felt. And by the time things eased off with my work hours, the patterns were in place. I didn't fight hard enough. I'm to blame as much as Anna.'

'And that's held you back, too, from taking a harder line on shared custody. The fact that you felt to blame.'

He nodded, even though she wouldn't see the movement in the dark. Maybe she would feel it. She seemed to feel and understand so much else without adequate words from him. He felt a rush of appreciation—the word was too weak, but he didn't have a stronger one—an appreciation for her that was so intense it left him winded and limp.

'Why are we talking about this?' He tightened his hold on her body.

'Because it's there in the air, in your heart, and you wanted to say it. Because it's relevant, with Josh in the next room for the first time since the divorce, with me here, too.'

'As easy as that?'

A moment's silence.

'Why should talking be so hard?' She stroked his chest with her fingertips, making lazy, seductive circles, exploring the texture of his skin and hair.

Why *should* talking be so hard?

His gut answered, rather than his rational mind. Because talking gave away information, and information was power. More than power. It was a weapon. He felt a sudden, terrible compulsion to talk to Miranda about his father, too, but pushed it back into that safe, hidden place deep inside him. Doing so wasn't hard. He'd had half a lifetime of practice.

The circles gave him the excuse he needed to take the easy way out. Hadn't he stretched his boundaries enough for one night? 'Why is talking hard?' His voice came out so lazy and seductive, it creaked. 'You have to ask? Because you're doing those sexy circles with your fingers. Distracting me. On purpose. And don't deny it.'

'Well…It didn't start out to be on purpose.'

'I'm telling you, talking's not just hard at this moment. It's getting to be bloody impossible…'

CHAPTER SEVEN

AT THREE o'clock in the morning, Miranda crept out of Nick's bedroom with her crumpled clothing held in a bundle against her chest. Nick was fast asleep and so was Josh. Miranda heard some sounds coming from the little boy's adjacent room—he was talking in his sleep. She slipped into the bathroom and dressed quickly, then let herself out onto the veranda.

Even at this hour, the tropical night was mild and almost warm. She hurried across the sandy ground to her own cabin, feeling a little uneasy at being out this late. There were a couple of reassuring lights around the place—one in the medical centre, one in the bathroom of a cabin she passed, one in the dining room that was kept on all night for security and to help keep away pests. The moon hung low in the western sky, disappearing from her view behind a tree's shaggy canopy as she came up the steps to her cabin's veranda.

OK.

Home.

Alone.

Happy?

For the first time since she and Nick had kissed, hours ago, she allowed herself to ask the question, and thought about it as she grabbed a drink of water and took off the clothes she'd only just put on, replacing them with a satiny slip of a nightgown that would have been way more seductive to strip off for her lover than the casual shorts and vest top. She had her wardrobe the wrong way around...

And there was something slightly wrong about being the one to get out of the bed, too. The man was supposed to do that, while the woman lay there wondering if and when she'd see him again.

But she felt good about it, she discovered.

About most of it. Leaving the cabin before dawn had been the practical thing to do, and the right thing to do for Josh's sake. And Nick couldn't duck out of seeing her again in the morning because she would pounce on him from behind a sandhill if he tried! As for leaping into bed with him in the first place, she felt dizzy over it, filled to the brim with emotion, thankful, sure.

It all seemed easy while she was still basking in the after-glow.

But something nagged at her as she lay in bed, struggling to find sleep. She thought about the way they'd talked after they'd first made love and the picture that had been blurred resolved into clear focus in her head.

Anna.

They'd made love, and then they'd talked about Anna.

Earlier, too, after Nick had brought her his mobile phone because his ex-wife had been on the line, what had he said? 'I was jealous.'

Just of Miranda's easy new friendship with Susie? Or, more importantly, of the intense, serious conversation Miranda had had with Anna?

Was it possible that he was still in love with her?

Nick and Miranda saw each other across the dining room at breakfast and instinctively looked away. Then they turned back at the same moment and smiled, and Miranda's lungs got that too-full feeling and she could hardly breathe.

He came up to her and stood about an inch too close, the kind of intimate distance that someone would have noticed if they'd been looking. 'Sleep well?'

'Um, no.'

'I don't think that's what you're supposed to say.'

'Sorry. I mean I slept like a baby.'

'And isn't that a myth—that babies sleep?'

There. Once again it was easy. Ice broken. Smiling at each other. Lovers and friends. Miranda's doubts were soon forgotten.

Her heart was still beating too fast. Her breathing hadn't quite returned to normal. Her feet still hovered a secret, blissful distance above the ground as if her sandals had wings. But those were the right feelings for now.

They had another wonderful day. Josh and Nick went snorkelling with a small group of parents and kids, supervised by qualified instructors. Josh wore a buoyancy vest and though he struggled with the snorkelling equipment and ended up just bobbing around beside his dad and occasionally peering at the reef through his face mask, he was hugely proud of his achievement.

He grinned from ear to ear as he came stomping out of the water in his flippers. 'Did you see me, Dr Carlisle?'

Miranda hadn't. She'd been doing some group physio and exercises with Susie in the activity room and had only just arrived down at the beach where the watersports were taking place. 'I bet you went so fast in those flippers!' she told him.

'And I wasn't scared and I didn't wheeze.'

'That's wonderful.' And I wish I could tell you to call me Miranda, but I know I can't...

She slept in Nick's bed just metres from Josh's room again that night, and this time she didn't leave to go back to her own cabin until almost dawn.

Julia Rabey spread her hands, at a loss for words. 'I don't know why this is happening, Dr Carlisle. I thought the sea air would be better for her. Less dust. And she usually does really well with swimming as long as she takes her preventative first.'

Mid-morning on Thursday, Kathryn was back at the medical centre in the throes of a second major asthma attack, unable to speak and looking panicky and stubborn. She'd been hooked up to a pulse oximeter and nebuliser mask, and was receiving a barrage of medication, but she was still struggling to breathe.

And she wasn't using her inhaler properly, Miranda noted. What was going on? For every strong and determined inhalation the nine-year-old took, there was another one that started out half-hearted, before the fear overtook the stubbornness and she made a belated bid to inhale the full dose.

She wants this attack...

She was scared of it, Miranda could see, but she was trying to force herself to go farther with it at the same time. Kids weren't very good actors, by and large. Good at hiding things sometimes, yes, but not good at putting on a performance. They were sloppy or inconsistent, or they went too far.

The oxygen level showing on the monitor began to rise. Kathryn's breathing was better now. No accessory muscle use, the way there had been at first. 'I can't breathe!' she said. 'Mummy, I can't *breathe*!'

No Best Actress Oscar for you this year, my love, Miranda thought.

'Yes, you can, sweetheart,' Julia said, tender and perplexed. 'You're sounding much better now. Can't you tell? You can!'

'I can't!'

Mrs Rabey looked at Miranda and shrugged. Kids were a mystery.

Miranda took her aside. Beth Stuart was sitting at the front desk, doing some paperwork, but it might be helpful if they brought her into this, too. 'Mrs Rabey, has she ever deliberately triggered or exaggerated an attack before?'

'No! Unless I just haven't seen it…But, no, she hates the bad attacks. They really scare her, and it's no wonder.'

'And you don't know of anything that's on her mind? Problems at school or at home? Money worries? Something that's happening to you or your husband that she could have picked up on?'

'I'm doubting my own perceptions now.' Julia shook her head. 'I'd have said there was nothing. We're a boringly happy family, as far as I'm concerned. But you're right. She wants the attention. And surely I'm giving it to her!'

'Maybe you're not the one she wants it from,' Beth came in quietly, surprising Miranda a little. Beth had such a successful line in lively chat, but apparently she was a good listener and observer, too.

'Well, she adores her dad,' Julia said. 'And we were all disappointed he couldn't come.' As part of Crocodile Creek Kids' Camp's policy of including healthy siblings when possible, Julia had Kathryn's younger brother Michael here as well. 'He had some company big-wig flying in this week and had to show him around. But surely she wouldn't *try* to make her asthma worse in the hope that he'd fly up? Barring an emergency, he really can't!'

'So maybe she's trying to create the emergency,' Beth said.

Mrs Rabey shook her head. 'That's too extreme. She's too sensible.' She repeated, 'And she hates the bad attacks.'

There was a bumping sound on the wooden ramp outside and the door opened to admit Charles in his wheelchair. 'I'm not here,' he said, perceiving that he might be interrupting something. 'I just need to borrow a stethoscope, a thermometer and some paracetamol. Won't be a moment. Beth, you could save time by grabbing everything for me.'

'Anything wrong?'

Charles winced. 'Not really. Lily's got a bug, or something. She's probably just incubating a cold. She didn't want breakfast this morning, and she's got a bit of a sore throat and a cough. She's still saying she wants to go and play on the beach.' His mouth tightened a little. 'And Jill's not out here yet, so it would be much easier if I could let Lily play, because I still have a lot to do before tomorrow and Saturday. But she feels warm to me.'

'We have a few children here that we really don't want getting sick,' Miranda pointed out.

'True. But she was probably incubating this yesterday so the damage is already done. You're right, though. She has to be kept away from the other kids now, even if it is just a mild cold. I'll have to send her home to Jill, or work something else out.'

Beth had now hunted up his list of items. 'Keep the paracetamol, but I want the stethoscope and the thermometer back!'

'Ten minutes,' Charles promised.

He manoeuvred his wheelchair in an expert pivot to face the door, but before Beth could dart in front to open it for him, the Allandales appeared, the parents looking highly anxious and ready to be angry, and Lauren sobbing with her hands over the lower half of her face.

'What's happened?' Beth said quickly. 'Where are you hurt, Lauren?'

'My face. I fell on the rocks. It really, really hurts.'

Miranda could see that it undoubtedly did. There was blood running between Lauren's fingers and dripping onto the medical centre floor. Julia had gone back to her daughter's bedside, still looking perplexed at the possibility that Kathryn might be deliberately triggering or exaggerating her attack.

'Let's have a proper look at you, sweetheart,' Beth was saying. 'Come through here. We'll get you all fixed up in no time. We've got Dr Wetherby and our lovely nurse Grace.'

'No, that's not acceptable,' Mr Allandale cut in sharply, as he understood what Beth was suggesting. 'Treat her here? No! We want you to call the helicopter service. You can put a dressing on it here and stop the bleeding, but you can't stitch it. It's on her face. She'll be scarred. She needs a plastic surgeon for this, at a major city hospital, not some rural jack of all trades with a carpet needle.'

'Don't worry, we threw out the carpet needles last year when we got in some smaller ones,' Charles said. Until now, he'd taken a back seat to what was going on.

He flashed a crinkly, white-teethed, let's-not-get-our-knickers-in-a-twist kind of grin that Miranda privately thought quite infectious and charming, especially given that he'd just had his medical credentials slammed in his direct hearing, but neither of the Allandale parents were in any mood for jokes or charm.

'That's ridiculous,' Mrs Allandale hissed.

'Let's take a look first, before we make any decisions,' Beth said, trying to settle the atmosphere.

'No,' said Rick Allandale. 'The decision's made.'

Charles didn't agree, Miranda could tell, but he didn't waste his time saying so. That evidently wasn't his style. 'Beth, run over and check on Lily for me, would you?' he said quietly. 'She's on her own in the cabin and I've already left her for too long.'

Beth nodded and didn't argue.

But when she went to leave, Kirsty Allandale said indignantly, 'Where are you going?'

'Dr Wetherby is going to have a look at Lauren.'

'You can't be a doctor!' She was looking at the wheelchair.

'Some people think so,' he replied mildly, 'but, in fact, I am. The medical director at Crocodile Creek Hospital, and the person ultimately responsible for making decisions on emergency medical evacuations for this whole region. Dr Carlisle, Lauren is your patient at home, so perhaps you'd come into the examination room with me?'

'Of course.'

He led the way, and the small cubicle simply didn't have room for both the Allandales at the same time, so Mrs Allandale came in while her husband stayed at the front desk, glowering.

The cut on Lauren's chin was a bad one, deep and untidy and embedded with grit. It definitely needed suturing after a thorough clean. With their ongoing anxiety about her health, Miranda could understand the parents' concern about scarring, but she could also understand that Charles couldn't possibly assign a hugely expensive helicopter evacuation to the city for purely cosmetic reasons.

'It has to be done here,' he said quietly to Miranda, after they'd retreated to the privacy of an office. 'Sending them across to Crocodile Creek Hospital wouldn't help.' He drawled, 'All my doctors over there are rural jacks of all trades, too. I mean, they're a brilliant bunch, but the Allandales won't believe that, and the fact is that none of them have specialised cosmetic surgery skills.'

'There is Nicholas Devlin,' she said slowly.

'Who? Oh, you mean Nick? Josh's dad?'

'That's right. He's a plastic and reconstructive surgeon at Royal Victoria Hospital in Melbourne.'

'I didn't even realise he was a doctor. He's kept that quiet!' Charles allowed himself a small chuckle.

'It might get you off the hook. I'm sure he'd be willing, and he has a very good reputation. This is such a wonderful place, and all the kids are having such a great time. I'd hate future camps to get marred by complaints or legal problems.'

Charles thought for a moment, then said decisively, 'Ask him. We're good at roping in stray doctors around here. Some of them even end up staying! While you're hunting him up, I'll clean out the wound and give Lauren a local, see if I can get the parents to be a bit more reasonable. Let's get this done.'

Miranda had a hard time ducking Mr Allandale's onslaught of demands. 'Dr Wetherby wants to talk to you first,' she said, to keep him at bay. There was no point in mentioning Nick and his specialist skills until she knew whether he was willing and able.

After some minutes of hunting, she found him returning from the beach with Josh, to get cleaned up for some quiet time before lunch. They both looked relaxed and—she hadn't consciously seen this before—incredibly alike. Dark hair, big boyish grins, tanned feet that moved nimbly on the sandy ground and seemed to relish their lack of shoes.

It was hard to break into their time together with a request for Nick's professional help, but if he was the man she believed him to be, she knew he'd want to give it.

'Of course,' he said, once she'd explained. 'But there's Josh.'

'There's a session just starting in the pottery room. Would he like that?'

Nick nodded. 'That's a good idea. Let me get him settled, and I'll be with you as soon as I can.'

Miranda heard raised voices as she came back up the ramp to the medical centre. Charles still spoke calmly, repeating his insistence that the helicopter service was not at their disposal, but the Allandales were both yelling in their attempt to argue their case.

'Hasn't our daughter been through enough?'

Miranda knew from experience that they wouldn't give up quickly. 'I've found a specialist,' she announced, before Dr Wetherby could repeat his quiet statement of the facts. The Allandales looked blank and suspicious, so she explained, 'He's a plastic and reconstructive surgeon at Royal Victoria Hospital. Nick Devlin.'

'But he's one of the parents.'

She smiled. 'We have a range of careers among our parents. A couple of them might surprise you! In this case, you couldn't have done better than Josh's dad.'

'I've talked to him,' Rick said. 'He didn't say he was a surgeon. We talked about chess.'

'But he is,' she assured them brightly, 'and he's willing to work on Lauren's injury. You're very lucky.' She emphasised the statement. 'It'll be so much better to have it done promptly on the spot, and it won't spoil her holiday.'

As if still suspicious that she might be putting one over them, the Allandales nodded, looked at each other and exchanged a short series of whispered phrases. 'As long as there's no delay,' Mrs Allandale said.

'And if you'll stand in on the procedure, Dr Carlisle,' her husband added.

'Of course, if you want me to.'

Charles raised his eyebrows at Miranda as if to ask, Is this typical?

Miranda spread her hands and shrugged. Yes, it was.

Rick slipped outside and soon had his mobile pressed to his ear, visible through the medical centre windows. He was phoning some contact of his in Melbourne to verify Nick's professional credentials, Miranda realised. Although the mistrustful action made her hackles rise, she accepted that she might have done the same thing if this had been her pretty and chronically ill teenage daughter. Like children, parents didn't always know how to behave! Kirsty had followed her husband outside, after a murmured excuse, and now they were talking.

Nick arrived just a few minutes later, walking with Beth. The latter told Charles, 'I took her temp. It's up a bit, but not much. Thirty-eight point three. I've given her the paracetamol and listened to her chest. There's some congestion building up, but it's probably viral so there's not a lot we can do. She'll shake it off in a day or two, she's such a sturdy little thing.'

He nodded. 'I expect she will. Is she on her own again?'

'I settled her on the couch with a book. She seemed happy. I can go back, if you like. She's so at home here, she'll run and find someone if she has any problems.'

'That's always what I'm afraid of, with Lily,' Charles answered. 'She could go out on the veranda in search of a tissue-box and strike up a lifelong friendship with the first person she sees, even if he had three heads and green teeth. No, I'll go. My professional skills have been roundly rejected, so I'm a free man.' He gave a wry grin and began to wheel himself towards the door.

Nick had already moved in the direction of the treatment room, where minor surgical procedures could be performed. He had no idea that his qualifications were still being investigated. 'Dr Stuart, can you give me a quick run-down on your set-up?' he said to Beth, who followed him quickly.

The Allandales came back inside and went directly to their daughter. 'Everything's going to be all right, sweetheart,' Kirsty said.

Meanwhile, in her hospital bed, Kathryn couldn't keep up the pretence that her attack was out of control. She was breathing much better, and lay back quietly against her pillows, tired out by the recent drama.

Miranda only had time to poke her head around the door, but bubbly, down-to-earth Grace was in attendance. They had an elderly man from the resort hotel in another bed, separated from Kathryn's by a partition jutting part way across the room and curtains drawn along tracks in the ceiling. The gentleman thought Grace was gorgeous, with her bouncy hair and twinkly blue eyes and just the teeniest bit of flirtiness in the way she talked to him, and it was making him feel better by the minute.

'I just want Daddy to come up here,' Miranda heard Kathryn say in a very small voice.

She went back to Nick and Lauren in the treatment room. 'Keep the parents out, can you?' he muttered to her. 'I hate having interested parties looking over my shoulder.'

'You'll have me, if you don't forbid it,' Miranda muttered back. 'They've asked if I can keep an eye on you.'

'Wha-a-a-t?'

'Don't take it personally. I'll pass you things. Can be quite useful, I can, when I want to be.'

'More cheekiness, Dr Carlisle?'

'I'm saving most of it.'

'Good…' He grinned at her and her heart melted.

In the end, the procedure itself created no drama. Charles had already administered the local anaesthetic, cleaned the cut and put a temporary dressing in place. Nick took a moment to plan his work, but once he actually began it he moved with a delicacy and speed that Miranda knew her own fingers could never have matched.

'We'll give you an antibiotic, Lauren, so

there's no danger of infection. The stitches will dissolve on their own. I'll take a look at it every day to make sure it's healing right.'

Lauren nodded. 'Here?' She'd taken the whole procedure calmly and patiently, with no complaints.

'I don't think we need to come here. We can do it on the beach, if you like.'

She managed a grin—no mean feat for a girl with a numb chin. 'That'd be good.'

She might be spoiled, especially in the company of her parents, but she'd spent enough time in hospitals to be stoical about them—and at the same time very happy to avoid yet another visit.

'Want to show Mum and Dad before we cover it up?' Nick asked, and Lauren nodded.

Miranda held her breath when the Allandales came in, but Nick explained what he'd done to minimise scarring and earned their complete confidence and a gushing level of gratitude in about a minute and a half. 'I don't know what we'd have done if you hadn't been here. Flown her to Brisbane in a chartered helicopter at our own expense. It would have been terrible,' Kirsty said.

When they'd gone, Nick said to Miranda, 'Should I have suggested they donate the cost of a charter flight to the new medical centre instead?'

She laughed. 'Only if you wanted to stir them up. You were great. Nobody wanted it to turn into a major incident, but it was heading in that direction.'

'Shall we go and pick up Josh?'

He ran his hand down her arm in a private, intimate gesture that made her heart sing, and a voice of hope inside her began to say, It's going to work out this time. It's the start of something wonderful. It's real.

Then she smelt the sunscreen on his neck and remembered the way she'd always felt when she played with the kids on the beach…and the way she'd felt when beach time ended.

CHAPTER EIGHT

'SHE was scared we were getting divorced!' Julia shook her head, reliving her mingled bemusement and relief at getting to the bottom of Kathryn's deliberately triggered and exaggerated attacks.

'But those attacks were real.' Miranda frowned. 'The second one, in particular. How did she trigger it?'

'Took the pillow slip and plastic cover off her pillow, the naughty girl, pressed her face into it and took several good big breaths.'

'That'd do it, yes,' Miranda agreed drily.

It was the reason Kathryn's pillows had a layer of plastic covering in the first place. No matter how thoroughly Julia might wash bedding and vacuum mattresses, any invisible dust, dander or mould spores trapped in pillows and upholstered seating triggered Kathryn's asthma if these items weren't covered in plastic.

'We're not getting divorced, I should tell you,' Julia said.

'What made her think it was a possibility?'

'Oh, she put two and two together and it came out wrong. We had an argument last week, Bruce and I, and she overheard. Unfortunately, she didn't hear the apology and compromise we reached at the end of it. And then he couldn't come up here, and I guess she thought the work commitment was just an excuse. Meanwhile, her best friend's parents have just separated, and she obviously thought that if it could happen to Megan, out of the blue, it could happen to her. I think we've sorted it out, now. I put her on the phone to Bruce and that helped.'

'You'll enjoy the rest of your stay much better now.'

'I wish we were having the full two weeks.'

Some people weren't. Miranda would say goodbye to three of her patients on Sunday morning and welcome three different ones on Sunday afternoon, although the rest were staying through for a second week.

The time had gone too fast. It was already Thursday afternoon, and Miranda expected that she or Nick would soon hear from Anna about her plans to fly up and take over Josh's care some time over the weekend.

'I want her mother to be managing badly. I want both her sisters to stay in Sydney and refuse to come down to Melbourne to help out,' Nick confessed darkly as they sat on the beach. 'Every hour that goes by without a phone call from her, I'm hoping it means she can't work something out. I'm hoping the flights will be full or there'll be a refuellers' strike, or something. She told me last night that she'd phone some time today about her plans, but she hasn't yet, for some reason, and I'm holding my breath. I want the extra week with him, and to hell with anyone else on the planet!'

As usual, after he'd spoken his darker thoughts, he withdrew a little. While Miranda chatted with a couple of parents, he walked down to the water's edge in brooding silence, as if replaying what he'd just said and regretting it.

He didn't need to.

Miranda loved his moments of honesty and flawed humanity. People weren't perfect. They gave her the jitters when they tried to be, because it wasn't natural. It was one of the things she'd hated about her childhood—the fact that her loving parents had tried too hard, had sheltered her too much, had made everything too safe and *nice.*

Of course Nick wanted another week with the son he was only just getting to know on a genuine, day-to-day level. She wouldn't say no to an airline refuellers' strike herself if it gave her another week of Nick's company.

By day and by night.

And if he was so unequivocal in not wanting Anna to come up, then surely he couldn't still have feelings for her.

Slathering herself with insect repellent in preparation for an evening of wildlife spotting later on, with Wallaby Island park head ranger Ben Chandler and his two junior staff, Miranda knew she'd have to fight the temptation to eat beside Nick and walk with him later, too, instead of parcelling out her time to patients and parents.

He understood, though. When she raised the subject as they lined up for spaghetti, he told her, 'I'll stick with Josh. You go wherever you need to go. Maybe later in our cabin...?'

'Definitely later in your cabin.'

But what was that saying about the best-laid plans…?

Josh was wildly excited about going out at night wearing a head torch and tramping through the bush. 'Where's Lily?' he asked, as he held out his plate to receive his meal. 'Isn't she coming? She has to come!'

'No, Lily isn't feeling well. She won't be coming tonight. And Garf would scare all the creatures, so he has to stay in camp, too.'

Nick had found out a little more about Lily. Charles Wetherby and Crocodile Creek Hospital's Director of Nursing Jill Shaw were acting as foster-parents, and her permanent future was still up in the air. He had the impression that Charles wasn't sure about his future with Jill either. They had marriage plans, apparently, but their relationship seemed to have been cobbled together for Lily's sake, which didn't sound like the healthiest of foundations.

'Couldn't she have her inhaler?' Josh was saying. 'Then she'd be OK.'

'Not asthma, Joshie.' He tended to assume that his own illness was a universal phenomenon. 'She has a cold.'

'Oh, OK.' He hopped back and forth from foot to foot and the tangle of spaghetti almost slid off the plate.

Nick had to anchor him in his seat over the meal with some stern words. 'Eat, Josh. Sit properly on your backside, please, and eat.' He hated saying it because it reminded him too much of his dad, and all those meals choked down stone cold, as a child, because he wasn't allowed to leave the table without presenting a thoroughly cleaned plate.

He hated saying it, too, because he hadn't seen fear and uncertainty in Josh's face in three days now, and if the sternness brought the fear back…

It did.

Not looking at him, Josh hunkered down over his plate and managed a few more reluctant mouthfuls of spaghetti bolognaise, but then he started only pretending to eat, pushing the strands of pasta around the plate and out to the sides and mashing them into shorter lengths so they would look like inedible scraps instead of real food.

Nick's father's attitudes were hard to shake, even after so many years. Kids did waste too much food. Perfectly good plates of nutritious dinner got scraped into bins to leave room for piled-high dessert. Parents became worn down by the constant need to say no to junk food and grew too soft.

'OK,' he heard a mother sigh at the next table. 'That'll do. Yes, go and get your ice cream…' She added half-heartedly, 'But have some fruit salad, too.'

The meals were good here, but it was hard to undo bad habits in a week or two. If getting kids to eat well had been hard in Nick's father's day, it was much harder now.

Hard to build a whole new relationship, too. 'Good grief, you're not really eating it, Josh,' he said in the end, far more sharply than he'd intended. 'So stop pretending. You're done.'

Josh put his fork down. After several seconds—building up his courage?—he asked in a small voice, 'Can I have dessert?'

There was half a meal still there on his plate!

'No, I'm sorry, not tonight,' Nick made himself say. 'If you're not hungry for spaghetti, then you're not hungry for ice cream.' Even though it was ridiculously tempting to agree to the ice cream just for the pleasure of seeing Josh's face light up.

'Yes, I am,' he insisted innocently. 'Mummy says I have two stomachs. My dinner stomach is full, but my dessert stomach is still empty.'

'Well, I'm afraid it's going to have to stay that way.'

Nick thought it was the right answer, but saying it was hard when all around them kids were coming back to the table with bowls of ice cream, fruit salad and jelly. He felt his non-custodial parent status like a dead weight—it was such a lonely role sometimes—and his deepening relationship with Josh like a fragile flower cradled in his hand.

What would he have to do to crush it? Not much.

'Does that mean I can leave the table?' Josh was too excited about the night walk to mind very much about dessert.

He wasn't a huge eater at the best of times, and his size and his asthma and his lack of appetite formed a triangle of cause and effect that Nick hadn't fully fathomed yet. If he ate better, would he fight the asthma more easily? If his lungs were clearer and bigger, would he feel hungrier?

'Yes, OK, you can leave. Scrape your plate and put it on the trolley with the others.'

Josh did so, looking too small as he stretched on tiptoe beside the scrap bin. Seconds later, he had joined a group of shrieking kids outside the dining room. One of them had a head torch on and was treating its beam like a light sabre, while the others ran back and forth in the darkness. 'I caught you, Josh! I caught you in the beam! And you, too, Danny!' Danny's round head, bald from his recent chemo, shone pale in the light.

One parent said, 'Shouldn't we get them to be quiet and stop running?'

Someone else answered, 'They're kids! It's what kids do. And I can't remember the last time my guy felt good enough to run!'

Miranda was eating at another table tonight, after she'd warned Nick that she needed to spend more of her public time with the other parents. 'I'd hate it if people began to make comments.'

As would he, but he missed her talent with his

son. No, forget Josh, he just *missed* her—her company, her smile, the way she smelled.

And she would somehow have managed to deliver the no-dinner-no-dessert message without his own sternness, Nick felt. She'd have smiled as she said it, with a mix of firmness and cheerfulness that he couldn't deliver naturally and couldn't fake either.

The mild father-and-son altercation was over now, but it had left an eddy of uncertainty that stayed with him as the park rangers drove up, introduced themselves, handed out extra torches and divided the night-walk participants into three groups. He and Josh ended up in Miranda's group mainly because that was the direction Josh ran in when the kids were finally asked to settle down.

Settling down was a bit of a stretch. Josh wasn't the only kid to be over-excited. There was shrieking and scuffling and giggling and hopping up and down.

'So do you want to see some animals tonight?' Ranger Ben asked.

A loud chorus of, 'Ye-e-s!'

'Tree kangaroos?'

'Yes!'

'Sugar gliders?'

'Yes!'

'Crocodiles?'

'Yes!'

'Well then, you'll have to…*be quiet*!'

At which point Josh and some of the other littler ones tried so hard to stifle their giggles and still their restless feet that they almost forgot to breathe.

Ah, yeah, breathing…

Fifteen minutes into the night walk, the attack built with a speed Nick hadn't seen at first hand since before his and Anna's separation. They were on the beach about half a kilometre from the main camp and just about to turn away from the water onto a forest trail when he first discovered Josh was having problems. He'd been darting around with a cat's curiosity, examining everything he found, trailing a piece of driftwood through the sand, and it was great, but then…

Ben was telling them about shearwaters nesting in the sand dunes. 'Some people call them mutton-birds because the early settlers used to think they tasted like mutton.'

Several of the kids still had to be shushed from time to time, and a couple of them were panting after running along the beach in loopy circles like puppies instead of listening to Ben. Others milled around on the edges of the group, stopping to examine a shell or wandering up towards the dunes at the top of the beach to kick up the loose sand.

Inevitably, Nick drifted into Miranda's company. They weren't talking much, but even just to walk along a beach beside her in silence gave him a unique, multi-stranded pleasure that he couldn't quite believe…and a kind of vertigo when he considered the implications. Forget those. He loved the smooth sheen on her bare legs in the moonlight, the casual swing of her ponytail, the way she broke the silence with a murmured comment meant just for him.

Josh appeared out of the darkness. 'Dad, I want my inhaler.' He'd circled back from another short foray up the beach, and his voice sounded strained and thick. The front of his shirt was speckled with something that Nick didn't have time to examine.

'Right here, Joshie.' He took off the daypack

he was wearing and crouched down on the sand at Josh-level while he unzipped it. 'You OK?'

He wasn't. Why even ask?

'I think I ran too much. And then I was—' wheeze '—trying too hard—' wheeze '—to be quiet.'

'No problem. Here we go.' Nick pushed the mouthpiece of the inhaler into the rubber sleeve on the spacer.

'And then…' Josh added slowly, then stopped. He appeared to be gathering his courage.

'What happened, Josh? Don't be scared to tell me. Please.' So it was still there, then, the fear and reluctance, beneath the bond they'd begun to establish this week…

Nick felt a spurt of self-disgust at his own naivety. Of course it was still there! You couldn't defeat five years of damaged history in a few days, and when you were the parent, it was up to you to keep pushing. With Miranda nearby, at least he didn't feel as if he was pushing totally alone.

'Come on, Joshie.' He gentled his voice and touched his son's shoulder.

'I found…someone's fire still warm…' Josh wheezed, 'and I was poking…in the ash…with a stick. It all came up suddenly…in my face… and I breathed.'

'Oh, hell,' Nick muttered. That was the speckled stuff on his shirt. White ash. It dusted his face and hair, too, and even his eyelashes. Oh hell…*hell*! 'Why on earth did you—?' He stopped and bit his anger back, mentally coaching himself.

Let it go. Don't mess this up.

There was no point in issuing recriminations. Josh was only five. Sometimes kids didn't think.

And Nick hadn't even seen. Not the fire, or Josh going near it. He'd been looking at Miranda instead. Now, too late, he saw the ring of stones and heap of grey ash and black coals up the beach behind them towards the dunes. A couple of beer bottles, too, and the discarded piece of driftwood Josh had used to poke the ash.

Damn! This was his fault!

The fact made him feel even worse about how close he'd come to yelling at his son in the middle of an asthma attack, with his son's doctor standing right by. Miranda. Where was she? Still with the group, he saw, answering a question from a parent. Hell, he couldn't claim her now…

At the edge of his awareness, he vaguely

heard Ben say, 'We're going to head into the rainforest next.'

And one of the other rangers was telling a child, 'No, hey, don't touch that, it's dead.'

And he didn't care if the group left them behind.

'OK, ready, Josh?' he said.

But Josh took the mouthpiece of the spacer away when Nick tried to put it to his lips. 'I feel sick. I breathed ash.'

'I know, but let's try your inhaler before we think about that.'

'I can't.'

'Joshie, we have to.'

He gave a small nod, but again waved the spacer away when Nick tried to put it to his mouth. 'Not yet.' They sat there for a moment, the sea washing in the background, while Josh struggled against nausea, and breathed and wheezed, still insisting every time Nick tried to get a dose of bronchodilator into him, 'I can't.' Finally, he managed several ineffectual puffs, but they had no visible effect.

Nick found a bottle of water in his daypack. 'Try this.' He gave Josh the bottle. 'Can you taste the ash in your mouth—is that the problem?

Is that what's making you feel sick and making your breathing go tight?'

Josh nodded. 'Tastes bad.' He took some water and spat it out, took some more and gulped it down, pausing twice between mouthfuls to breathe. His condition was getting worse, his reactions more panicky. He had to accept the inhaler, even if he didn't want to. 'Just do it, Josh! Come on!' The sharp words came more from fear than anger, but his son couldn't know that.

Josh tried, then leaned over the sand and lost the small amount of dinner he'd had an hour earlier. Nick's stomach knotted tighter with guilt. Should he have listened to Josh and waited longer to try the inhaler, or had he been right to push? Whatever the case, he shouldn't have yelled about it.

Suddenly, Miranda was there. 'I saw you drop back from the group. I'm sorry, someone was talking to me and I couldn't get away.'

Nick looked up the beach and discovered the others disappearing behind the dunes and into the forest. 'Have we been sitting here—?'

'A few minutes, that's all. Six or seven, I guess.

I told Ben not to wait. The other kids have settled down now. Ben is good with them. One of them just found a dead shearwater. Josh, how are you doing, sweetheart?'

'Joshie, we have to try again with the inhaler.' Nick looked up at Miranda again. 'He breathed in a whole lungful of ash. Someone had a fire here this afternoon.'

'Without a permit, I would think.'

'Apparently.' He fingered some of the stuff on Josh's shirt. 'It's so fine, finer than dust. Hell!'

Josh nodded at Nick and this time reached willingly for the inhaler, whether because the nausea had now subsided or the squeezed chest had grown worse, Nick couldn't tell. He looked as pale as the sand. Paler. And so heartbreakingly little and thin.

'Remember how we do this, Josh,' Miranda coached him. 'You know. Hold it to your mouth, and one, two, three. That's better…'

But Josh shook his head. His breathing wasn't better.

Nick saw the accessory chest muscles coming into play with the kind of effort common after heavy exertion—the muscles between the ribs, across the chest and below the sternum. You saw it in runners or cyclists at the end of a long race, but you didn't want to see it in an asthmatic child at rest.

'I don't like sitting on the beach like this,' he muttered to Miranda. Josh was too strongly focused on his struggle to breathe to listen. 'We're, what, ten or fifteen minutes' walk from the medical centre by now?'

'About that. And I don't have much equipment with me. Only my stethoscope, in my daypack. I want to have a listen to him.' She swung the pack off her shoulders and pulled the stethoscope out. 'Joshie, let's try some more puffs to make you feel better, before we get moving.'

More breaths, more counting, more puffs.

But if they had an effect, it didn't show.

Miranda listened with her stethoscope in several places, her face carefully not telegraphing to Josh what she thought. 'Medical centre,' she said. 'Play it safe. I have my mobile, I'll call them, see if someone can send one of those golf buggy things.'

'This seems to be building faster and much worse than the one he had at the airport on Sunday.'

'I think so, too.'

'That ash. I should have seen what he was doing. I've been trying not to wrap him in cotton wool this week.' The way Anna did, far too much. Damn it, Anna wasn't relevant now. 'But maybe I've gone too far the—'

'It doesn't matter,' she cut in. 'Save it. It's not your fault.'

Anna wouldn't agree.

Nick knew that as well as he knew his own name, but didn't have time to think about it. He did think about the fact that she hadn't phoned yet with news of her plans, then realised he'd left his mobile in the pocket of his other shorts. Hell! Still, the last thing he wanted was to get her on the line now and listen to her litany of recriminations. He'd call from the medical centre when Josh's attack had begun to settle down.

'Let me carry him,' he said. 'Joshie?'

Josh held up his arms at once. His nostrils were flaring with every attempt at a breath, and as they made their way back along the beach, Nick could barely hear him wheezing. He'd forgotten how terrifying that was. The wheezing was bad enough, but when Josh's lungs were too constricted to give off any whistles or rales at all, it was even scarier.

'Don't…hold me…so tight.'

'I'm trying not to.' His hold was as loose as he could make it, low around Josh's hips and well away from the muscles he needed for breathing, but Josh reacted against anything that felt like further constriction.

And Nick was almost running now. Miranda had spoken some rapid phrases into her mobile, which, thank heaven, had still been in range. 'They'll be ready for us,' she told him. 'The hotel is sending a buggy up, but we might get there first.'

She kept up with him, the buggy didn't appear in time, and they reached the medical centre after several minutes of thigh-burning effort. As they came up the ramp, Nick had a second fleeting thought that he should phone Anna to tell her what was happening.

Should he? Or would it be better for her not to know until the crisis was over? More importantly, would it be better for Josh? He had a flash of rebellious certainty that Josh's first serious asthma attack without Anna wailing and wringing her hands over him would actually do all three of them good.

And yet he knew Anna wouldn't thank him for keeping her in the dark. This was her son...

A moment later the immediacy of Josh's attack took over and the question was pushed from his mind.

The doctor and nurse working the twelve-hour overnight shift tonight were people neither Miranda nor Nick had yet met, although he had a vague awareness that they'd been at the beach bonfire the other night. The doctor introduced herself as Janey Stafford, and the nurse was Marcia someone. Her last name fled from Nick's head as soon as he heard it and he didn't take his eyes off Josh long enough to look at her badge.

He felt his usual temptation to pull rank, the way his father would have done: 'I am a first-class passenger...I have paid a premium for this service...I am the sole proprietor of this company.' Those blustering phrases had been a regular feature throughout Nick's childhood, until he was sixteen, and it had killed his father when he'd been unable to use them any more.

Literally killed him, Nick sometimes thought.

His own repertoire of bluster would have been

slightly different, although it amounted to the same thing.

I am a senior surgeon...I have been published in eight different medical journals in the past two years alone...I probably out-earn you by a six-figure margin.

But he never said any of those things. He swallowed them back no matter how much they burned to spill out, even in a situation like this when his heart was beating too fast and his own breathing was almost as shallow as Josh's, because in his experience that kind of bullying backfired and you always paid.

'Just get him oxygen and a nebuliser and get him breathing.' He wasn't ordering, he was begging.

Neither doctor nor nurse stalled. 'Yep, into a bed, little guy,' Dr Stafford said. 'Let's fix you up nice and fast.'

She whipped out a stethoscope, but Miranda said, 'Can I? Do you mind? He's my patient at home. I had a listen on the beach, I'll know if there's been any change.'

'Of course. I'll take a back seat.'

'You know what I'll need for him.' She already

had her own stethoscope in her hand. 'Can we take him through to a bed right now?'

'Yes. Take one of the last two on the left. We have paediatric equipment on hand by those beds.'

Nick forced himself to stay out of their way, to be Josh's father instead of a doctor, even though every instinct inside him said it wasn't enough. 'Feeling safer now that you're here?' he asked him quietly.

Josh nodded, but it was token. 'Want water.' The words were feeble, barely counting as speech. Nick wouldn't have known what he was saying if he hadn't already guessed that his son's mouth must be painfully bitter and dry.

'Can we get him some water? He wants to rinse his mouth again.'

He could barely manage to get it in his mouth, and spat it out at once in favour of his struggle for breath. He was tiring fast, working those accessory muscles harder, wearing them out to little effect.

Josh thought of hospitals as good places— places that helped him to breathe again—but the struggle for air was so immediate and the body's panicked response so primal and physical, he wouldn't relax on the strength of a promise. He needed the reality, the oxygen going into his lungs, the medication opening those constricted airways.

He'd begun to look blue around the mouth.

'You're OK, Josh. You're fine.'

Where were some better words? Josh wasn't fine, he was already approaching exhaustion, drowsy and confused, eyes closed, all effort poured into the struggle for air, showing all the signs of a critical attack. He mouthed something vague that Nick couldn't make out.

Not Monday? Not Mummy?

What had he said? How much did he wish that Mummy was here? Mummy with her soft, familiar body and her warm voice, instead of this Dad person Josh hadn't spent enough time with, who had laid down the law over dinner and dessert, who'd tried to shove the spacer into his mouth when he hadn't wanted it, and who was much better at digging sand tunnels than at giving hugs.

Lord, he should call Anna, he knew he should, but he hated the idea.

'You're going to be fine,' he repeated, making the promise to himself as much as to his son.

Miranda and Janey had the nebuliser ready, but it wasn't yet hooked up. According to the pulse oximeter clipped to Josh's finger, his blood oxygen level was hovering at eighty-eight per cent, when anything below the high nineties started to raise concerns, and below ninety indicated a critical attack. His heart rate was markedly fast. They had to get an improvement in his condition soon.

Nick cracked.

'Listen, Dr Stafford.' His voice was harsh enough to hurt his own throat. 'I'm not sure if you know this, but I'm a surgeon—plastic and reconstructive—at Royal Victoria Hospital. I work with some of the best people in the damned country.'

He saw Miranda's quick, covert glance in his direction but couldn't read it. Right now, he didn't care what she thought, didn't care about the lingering, unresolved anger against his father, or anything else. He just wanted some power and control in this situation, and to find a belief that his presence was good for Josh.

'I bailed you lot out today,' he went on, 'with some work on a patient's face that no one here could have done as neatly or as fast. I expect the best treatment in the world for my son, and I'll know immediately if I'm not getting it. That's not a threat, but you can bet your life it's a promise! Get him breathing again. Just do it.'

Damn, damn…

Why did I do that?

'We're doing it, Dr Devlin,' Janey said calmly. 'Josh, you know how this works, don't you, sweetheart? Just breathe as normally and steadily as you can.'

But he was too far gone to respond. The breathing had to come from his body's reflexes at this point. Miranda was watching him, assessing his response. What was she thinking?

'I'm going to put in a drip right now,' she said. 'He may not tolerate corticosteroids orally, although we'll try.'

'Aminophylline?' Nick asked.

'Not yet. Antibiotics pretty soon, though, as a precaution, because of that ash in his lungs.'

'What else?'

'Nebulised salbutamol, IV salbutamol and adrenaline if he needs it.'

'Why wait on the aminophylline?'

'Because his heart didn't like it last time, so we'll avoid it if we can.'

'He's reached this point before?'

'Worse, actually.'

'Anna never told me…'

'You were away at a conference.'

'Don't make me the bad guy, Miranda.'

'I'm not.' She turned away from him, to the tray of IV equipment Janey had brought.

The strength ebbed from Nick's legs without warning, hard on the heels of the realisation that he was arguing about past events in his marriage with a woman he, yes, loved…just say it, Nick, even if it doesn't make sense, don't mess around with complexities tonight, you love her—still—always…while his son was fighting for his life.

He sat beside Josh's bed and took his little hand. 'Dad's here, Joshie.' He spoke calmly, pinning himself to hope and trust—the trust he had to have, as a doctor, in the power of medicine, the trust he had to have in his own ability not to mess this up. 'Dr Carlisle is going to get you breathing again.'

The words felt too pointless so he stopped saying them, and just sat there thinking, *I love you, I love you, I love you,* over and over as if Josh could feel his thoughts through their joined hands.

And Miranda, too? Did she know, without words, how he felt?

She swabbed alcohol over the back of Josh's hand and looked for a vein, but her first attempt with the needle failed and Josh winced and whimpered a tiny, breathless whimper, while Miranda herself made a sound of distress. She tightened a strap across his upper arm and swabbed the crook of his elbow instead. 'This looks better. We'll get it.'

And this time the needle went in at her first try. Deftly, she slid the cannula along the vein, taped it in place, attached the plastic tubing, and the medication began to run in through the port, joining the saline dripping from the bag suspended on a stand nearby. The neat, quiet way she worked nourished something inside him.

No fuss.

In the context of Josh's health, Nick was so sick of fuss.

He took Miranda aside as soon as she had a moment to spare. 'Tell me about his heart, that other time.'

'It was already beating too fast, and the aminophylline made it beat faster.'

'That's the explanation you'd give to a layman, not to another doctor!'

'Nick, this isn't something I want you to worry about now. But all right…' She reeled off a more technical answer, laced with figures and abbreviations. 'Did that help?'

'Hell knows,' he admitted honestly. 'If…if none of this works, Miranda…'

'It will work,' she said crisply. 'We're treating it as critical and, based on past attacks, he'll respond. Please, don't make Anna's mistake and let him see how worried you are.'

'You're right,' he muttered. 'Hell, you're right.' The sense of powerlessness gripped him again and all he could do was sit there and wait and hope.

It was such a long night.

Nick sat beside Josh for six straight hours, watching his son's numbers slowly improve—blessedly without the need for the next level of medication. Once the clock's hour hand hit midnight, he began to doze a little, only to snap awake again every few minutes with his attention instantly riveted to his son or the monitors.

Josh's heart rate slowed, his blood oxygen level went up, that painful, exhausting effort of the accessory chest muscles eased and his son's sleep changed from near-coma to something much more nourishing and natural. Josh was totally exhausted. He wouldn't wake up any time soon.

'He's looking a lot better,' Miranda said softly.

'You're still here?' His voice creaked. 'I thought you'd gone.' He'd been aware of her presence and that of a couple of staff, as well as the regular observations and lines in Josh's notes, some background conversation in low voices, responses to a patient call button because they had a couple of other patients in the four-bed room next door.

'I was just grabbing some tea,' she answered. 'You've had nothing, Nick. Janey's telling us both to go back to our cabins and get some sleep.'

'You should.'

'So should you. Have you phoned Anna?'

He swore.

No, he hadn't.

'She'll think it was deliberate,' he said.

'And was it?'

'Partly. Half. Yes. Yes, it was. She was supposed to phone me today. She didn't, I don't know why, and I thought about phoning her, I kept thinking about it, and thinking, No, not yet.'

'It's late. What do you want to do?'

He was too tired for anything other than naked honesty. 'I want to be with you…'

'Me…' She tilted her head, folded her arms across her chest. The movement softened her shoulders and lifted her breasts and he felt a stirring of desire that jarred him in this context, even though at the same time it felt right.

'Could we take a break?' he said.

'Oh, please, yes…'

'My mobile's in my cabin. She'll have left messages.'

'Right.' Miranda gave a short, jerky nod and took a breath. 'You'll phone her now?'

'Let me see what messages she's left. She'd have wanted to fly up here tonight if I'd told her about this earlier.' He thought for a moment, and added, 'No, she'd never have made it in time, even if I'd called her from the beach. She'd have caught the first flight in the morning, though. I— I know at some level my not phoning—forgetting to and resisting it and putting it off—was deliberate. Freudian.' Nick laughed cynically at his use of such a word.

'Oh, Nick...' Miranda whispered in a tight voice.

'I wanted to see if it was better for Josh that way. If he panicked less. If he did better with me around. I didn't want her rushing in and shutting me out. Oh, hell, why do I always tell you this stuff?'

He closed his eyes, appalled by his own mixed motivations, then felt Miranda's hand soft and warm on his arm. 'Let's talk,' she said quietly.

CHAPTER NINE

Miranda had a quiet word with Janey and Marcia, then she and Nick left the medical centre and took the cool, silent walk across to his cabin. He didn't touch her, and she somehow knew he needed to deal with Anna's probable phone messages first, before they talked or did anything else.

Did he still have feelings for her, or was her presence in so many of their conversations about something else?

And then maybe he wouldn't want to talk, in the end. Maybe those walls would come back up and he'd push her away. She could see all the possible bad endings leading off into the night, but still she walked beside him because something in her heart—and in his?—didn't allow her to do anything else.

He went straight for the mobile phone on the kitchen bench-top once they were inside. 'Yes, she called. Several times.' He read a text. 'Wants me to phone as soon as I get this, no matter how late it is.'

'Does she mean that? It's nearly three in the morning.'

He shrugged. 'I'd better take her at her word.'

'You'll tell her about Josh's attack?'

'From any angle, it seems the right thing to do. I should have done it hours ago, as soon as we got to the medical centre. I shouldn't have put it off. There's no excuse. She's his mother.'

But he was still fighting the idea, she thought. He certainly didn't *want* to talk to her. His body was knotted tight as his thumb worked the numbers on the phone. He listened for a moment, then reported, 'Switched off or out of range.' He waited, then delivered a stilted message. 'It's Nick. Call back as soon as you can, any time. I got your messages.'

He flipped the phone shut and shoved it into his pocket, turning to Miranda as he did so. He had a helpless expression on his face that at once made her want to go up to him, kiss him, say all the right things—if she only knew what those were, if only she knew whether he wanted to hear them.

But she didn't know, so she waited, and Nick spoke instead. 'I'm wiped.'

'So let's sit.'

'I want to go back to Josh soon.'

'He's sleeping. If he wakes up and wants you, Janey or Marcia will let you know straight away. Let me make you some hot chocolate or something. Do you have any?'

'In the kitchen, on the bench,' he said vaguely. 'Josh would live on the stuff if he was allowed to.'

She nudged him in the direction of the couch and he laughed and told her, 'I'm as helpless as a baby. You'll have to undress me next.'

'Well, I always like doing that…'

He laughed again, then added, 'Holding yourself together is bloody tiring!'

'So stop the holding.'

'Yeah? How's that done?'

'Starts with the hot chocolate and a woman in your arms.'

'Has to be the right woman.'

'True.'

And the right woman is me…I think, I want…but there's a long way to go yet…

She made two mugs of hot chocolate in the microwave and brought them over to the couch, where they sat and sipped in silence. She somehow knew it was better to wait for him, not to bother him with questions or words he might not want to hear tonight.

I'm not sure where we go from here, Nick. We told each other I love you *ten years ago. I think we've discovered all of that intensity again this week, but can we really push through everything that's in the way?*

'Do you know, my father's business went belly up eight months before he told us?' Nick said, when she was still following the implications of what had never, not for a moment, been simply an end-of-exams one-night stand, or, this week, a holiday fling.

The direction that his thoughts had taken surprised her into saying, 'You haven't told me anything about your father.'

'No. Well.'

'You get your reticence from him?' she teased lightly.

'Come here.' He held out his arm to pull her close to him on the couch. Two empty mugs now sat on the coffee-table in front of them.

She went, having no choice about it. There was a night-follows-day inevitability about everything she felt for Nick Devlin, and if she was ever going to fight it, now wasn't the time.

He held her as if he needed her down to his bones, turning to bury his face against her neck, wrapping his arms tight, breathing against her body, twisting her so they were locked together. 'My dad was such a brute,' he said, his voice rusty and reluctant. 'But he was harder on himself than on any of us. I still believe some of the things he taught us, and it's so hard to know what to keep and what to discard. I do keep too much to myself. I am too scared of really getting close. I've never hit Josh, but—'

The words startled her into speech. 'Your father hit you?'

'He believed it was the right thing to do. I don't think he liked it. He *administered* it, you know? Like medicine. Planned and measured doses, on appropriate body parts, for selected offences. But he punished himself, too. Hell, did he ever punish himself! For eleven months, when I was sixteen, he struggled with the downturn in his business, not telling a soul—not my mother, not his employees—getting deeper into debt, putting together these doomed strategies to bail the company out, hiding paperwork, doing everything in secret because it wasn't a man's role to talk or seek help or share burdens. He shouldered everything on his own.'

'I expect those planned and measured doses of his got bigger and more frequent, though.'

Silence. 'Yes. That obvious?'

'From the outside.'

'So you're saying I shouldn't credit him with any courage? That he was taking out his failure on us as much as on himself?'

'Oh, Nick, I wouldn't presume to make those kinds of judgements. Not without knowing more.'

'And, of course, he couldn't keep it to himself forever. The whole thing came crashing down and he lost the business. Even then, he managed not to tell us until there was no choice. He ended up working the cash register at a garage for the last three years of his life, ringing up money for petrol and oil changes. He felt the humiliation and failure of it every minute of every day, but he didn't talk about that either. He put up this angry, resentful wall so thick that I don't think my mother could ever say to him, "You're still a man in my eyes." I don't think they ever said that they loved each other. Not even when he was in the cardiac unit with his life hanging by a thread.'

'He didn't make it, did he?'

'No, he died before they could get him stable enough for surgery.'

'Were you there?'

'No. By the time my mother phoned from the hospital…' His voice went husky and trailed off. 'I got there half an hour later. Practically cried on a nurse's shoulder. I was nineteen. She was like you, a bit. Warm. Her heart in her eyes.'

'Oh, Nick.'

'Your—your parents are both still alive, aren't they?'

'Yes,' she answered, seeing his desperate attempt to drag the conversation away from himself, away from the starkness of what he'd already said. She suspected he wouldn't succeed—that there was a lot more—but gave him what he wanted, the safety of hearing her share some vulnerability, too. 'They're in their seventies now. Trundling around the country in a caravan.'

'Are you close to them?'

'I am. They're lovely. I was an only child, though, and they were already in their late thirties when I was born. They worried a lot. They didn't even want me to have a pet in case it died and broke my heart. It was a bit claustro-phobic sometimes. I wanted…'

'More freedom?'

'More people to laugh with. More people to love.'

That was the word that made the seismic shift.

'Oh, lord. Oh, hell. That's what it's all about, isn't it? Love. I—I expect Mum might have tried to say it—I love you, to Dad—but he wouldn't have wanted to hear it from her.'

'No? Not even when he was so ill?'

'I honestly think his heart attack came from the pressure of feeling he'd failed in the real world and having no other measure of his own worth than that kind of financial success. And no outlet. For anything. Raising three sons didn't count, maintaining a marriage didn't count, all the years he had supported us, paid for private education, kept us in a comfortable house—none of that counted.'

'Why are you telling me this now, Nick, do you think?' she whispered. He was still holding her and she could feel the tension in him, still as tight as stretched wire after the long night of vigil over Josh's asthma.

'Because every time I catch myself echoing his behaviour, staying silent instead of talking, shouldering things alone instead of sharing… sharing so much with you this week, and years ago has felt—' But he broke off, picked up where he'd been going before. 'You know, yelling when I shouldn't, being strict and angry with Josh when maybe he needs something different and I'm being blind to it—I think about Dad and I have this mix of anger and pity and regret…' His voice cracked again. 'He died when there was so much left that I hadn't said…and that he hadn't said…and that we probably wouldn't ever have said, either of us, even if he'd lived another thirty years. And that's so sad and so wrong.'

He sobbed against her body, big, shuddery, rusty sobs that he couldn't control and that came from so far down inside him Miranda knew they'd taken him totally by surprise, even though she'd seen them coming for a while. Through that desperate little digression about her parents. For hours, in hindsight, ever since Josh had started wheezing on the beach and Nick had felt so powerless.

'It's all right. It's OK,' she whispered.

You just had to say it, no matter how inadequate it was.

It's OK, because I'm here.

Which was pretty arrogant, if you thought about it. Did she really have any power at all to help him? Was she at all important?

She kissed his tears away before they fell, and the shudders stopped and the sobs ebbed until he was quiet. 'Nick…?' she ventured.

'No.'

'No?'

'You're going to— And I don't want it. Questions. Commentary.'

'That's not…' Fair.

Pointless to say it. She had no expectation that he'd be fair, when he was already reeling and numb with shock at having made himself so vulnerable.

'I just want to feel you and taste you and kiss

you and forget,' he said. 'Can we do that, instead, Miranda? I'm…glad you're here.'

Even this, she knew, was a huge admission, huge progress.

'Yes, we can do that,' she whispered, and barely got out the words before his mouth found hers.

He didn't kiss her like a vulnerable man, he kissed her with a strength and certainty that made her stomach flip and the blood beat in her ears. He claimed her body with every touch, his fingers brushing across her tightened nipples through her clothing, his weight pressing against her. He muttered her name, over and over, and even though he didn't tell her he loved her, she believed that he did.

She *had* to believe it.

On any other night, it would have gone much further, with Nick leading the way, grabbing her and pulling her towards the heights. They would have ended up in bed together in the dark within minutes, their bodies pressed skin to skin, setting each other on fire with their hands and their mouths. Miranda wanted it. Her body throbbed for it. But she didn't think it wasn't going to happen.

Sure enough, he tore himself away at the most

impossible moment, just when she'd begun to think that it would be the best thing they could possibly do—make love, give themselves to each other and forget everything else.

'I can't do this.' He slumped against the back of the couch and covered his face with his arm.

'I want you to,' she whispered.

'I'm a mess.'

'This isn't messy.'

Silently, he shook his head, still hiding his eyes, and Miranda faced her choices. Let him go, or…

No, she wasn't going to let him go tonight. She wasn't going to let him run from his own nakedness. She wasn't going to be *nice*.

'This is not messy,' she repeated softly. 'This is right. This is us. Making love. Because we want each other. Because we love each other. Because Josh is safe and we've had a terrible night.'

She didn't wait for him to answer. And she didn't care if he couldn't tell her that he loved her in return. Better to play with the kids on the beach and then say goodbye, rather than not play with them at all. Well, Shakespeare said it better. To have loved and lost…

She caressed his arm and drew it gently away

from his face and down to his side. Then she straddled him on the couch, her knees on either side of his thighs and her body poised over him. She began to kiss him again, bending to find his mouth, anchoring it right where she wanted it with the curve of her palm against his jaw.

'It's OK,' she whispered. 'It really is.'

Because if they didn't do this, she wasn't convinced there was any way…any chance…that they'd find a connection when morning came. He'd be lost to her. He wouldn't know how much she cared. Words weren't enough. Words weren't nearly as powerful and irrevocable as he thought.

'Miranda…' His voice was edgy, tense.

'That's not the way to say my name. Say it how you said it before.' She stroked his neck and ran her fingers through his hair.

'Miranda…'

'That's better. Getting better.' She kissed him more deeply, teasing him with her parted lips and the languorous brush of her tongue.

He groaned and pushed on her shoulders, still fighting her and fighting himself, but the movement turned into a caress. His hands slipped down her body and closed over her breasts, cupping them through her clothing, stroking them until her nipples burned.

She peeled off her top, unhooked her bra and dropped both garments on the floor. He barely waited. His hands were there ready to brush over her breasts again at once. He wasn't fighting any more.

'Oh, Nick…' But she'd claimed victory too soon. 'I can't.'

He already was.

She didn't listen to his protest but began to unfasten the buttons on his shirt instead, opening it to run her hands over the hard heat of his chest. He groaned again, and she almost thought he was shaking. 'Miranda…'

If he was asking her to stop, his body was saying something very different. She felt the upward thrust of his hips against her crotch and then he pulled her against him and her breasts pressed into his chest. 'OK,' he whispered. 'You win.'

Only now did he take control, twisting so that he could lay her against the couch, her head pillowed against one of the bright cushions that sat against the arm. He kissed the shallow valley between her breasts, then moved his mouth down as he unfastened her shorts and dragged them over her hips and down her legs. Her whole body was throbbing, wanting him.

He discarded his own clothing and found the protection they needed with the same sinuous speed, and when he came back to bury his face in her neck, his eyes were closed. She lifted her hips and moved them against his body, asking for him, needing him. He gave her what she wanted, and they were locked together until she lost all sense of time and space. Every touch and every movement delivered a message of love, if he wanted to hear it.

But there was no lazy aftermath like they'd had the past two nights.

'I have to get back to Josh.' Nick dragged himself away and onto his feet, pacing halfway across the room in a matter of seconds as if needing to put in the most distance he could.

He found his discarded clothing on the floor and dressed before Miranda had even moved. She struggled to catch up to him, found her underclothing and her shorts but couldn't find her top until Nick held it out for her.

'I'll walk you to your cabin first,' he said. 'Don't argue, Miranda, will you?'

'If you don't want me to.' She smiled. 'Although I think I've just proved I can put on a pretty good argument if I have to.'

'I'm not playing games.' His mouth looked tight and tired, and so did his eyes.

'I know that.' She wanted to reach up and touch his face, smooth the tension away, but sensed that he wouldn't let her. He'd already begun to push her away and, even though she'd expected it, the speed of it and the reality of it still hurt.

'Thank you.'

'You don't need to thank me, Nick.'

But he said it again when they reached the steps up to her veranda. 'Thank you, Miranda.'

He squeezed her hands but didn't kiss her, and she went inside not knowing if he'd ever let her get close to him again. Anna would probably arrive on the weekend. Was Anna important? Whether she was or she wasn't, Nick would be going home. Miranda would be Josh's doctor again, and it would be so easy for Nick to run away from anything more than that, if he wanted to. She watched him from the cabin window as he walked across to the medical centre, his height and strength doing nothing to take away from the solitary appearance of his figure receding into the darkness.

'I'm not going to let him push me away this time,' she vowed out loud. 'Whatever it takes, I'm not.'

Josh looked so much better when Miranda went in to see him at seven in the morning, you would never have known how ill he'd been ten hours earlier. He wanted breakfast, and when it arrived from the camp kitchen on a tray, with lids covering the dishes, he lifted the lids and greeted each item as if it were a birthday gift.

'Strawberry yoghurt! Eggs and bacon and hash browns! Banana muffin!' He ate it all, then wanted to know, 'When am I going back to my cabin?'

'Sweetheart, not yet,' Miranda had to say. His chest didn't yet sound as clear as she wanted it to be, and she knew how hard it would be for Josh to stay quiet once he was back in the company of the other children. 'Maybe this afternoon, but I'll still want to keep a close eye on you.'

'Oh, I always have a close eye on me,' Josh said. 'Mummy keeps very close eyes.' Was that a sigh?

'I bet she does,' Miranda said neutrally. 'She loves you very much.'

Where was Nick?

Josh must have read her mind. 'Dad's gone to get breakfast.'

'Oh, OK.'

She wanted to see him, wanted eye contact, wanted to know what kind of a fight she was facing today, what kind of a future she had to prepare for. The promise she'd made to herself in the early hours of the morning seemed glib now. Sometimes one person's determination wasn't enough.

'It takes two,' she said under her breath, and in the bright light of day, after too little sleep, she didn't know if there were two people who really wanted this.

'Nick!' Anna reached him on the phone as he sat in the camp dining hall, gulping down his breakfast so he could get back to Josh.

'What's happening, Anna?'

'I'm flying up today.'

'Today?'

'Louise and Bron are here.' Anna's sisters. Anna herself was the middle one of the three. 'Both of them.' She gave a laugh, sounding a little bemused about it. 'They flew down from Sydney on Wednesday afternoon, and they're going to look after Mum for ten days. I'm a bit...' The sentence trailed off. Anna didn't seem to know how she felt about her sisters being there.

'I wasn't expecting you until the weekend. Sunday.'

'So, yippee,' she drawled, 'you're off the hook two days early.'

'That's not what I meant, damn it, and you know it.'

'You would have known my plans sooner if you'd returned my calls. I was getting frantic last night. I could have killed you.'

'And you could have called sooner. I was waiting half the day.'

'I—I know. I'm sorry about that. How is Josh? Is he fine? Is he still having a good time? Is he eating right? I—It feels weird being this out of touch. Having to ask these questions. Not seeing him. Like vertigo.'

And, of course, he had to tell her, no point in trying to hedge or soften it. Even knowing this, he said the words with slow reluctance. 'He had a pretty major attack last night.'

'Pretty major? What does that mean?'

Her slight air of bewilderment—vertigo, she'd just called it—disappeared. She was instantly on the alert, ready to judge him and find him wanting. He could feel the sizzle of her sudden anger down the phone like electricity, and in an odd way it put both of them on more solid ground.

Because it was so familiar.

And because he knew, now, what he wanted instead.

'How the hell could that happen with Miranda around? A *pretty major* attack?' She swore. 'How major? When? What did you do, Nick?'

'Took him to the medical centre.' There! At the hint of a suggestion that it might be his fault, he'd immediately distanced himself, withdrawn, given her the bare minimum.

'You know that's not what I mean!' Her voice rose higher. 'Why won't you ever give me the details?'

Because anything I say you turn around and

use as a weapon, so I use weapons of my own—
silence and withdrawal.

He wouldn't have said it, even though he'd started to understand it so much better, but she didn't wait for his answer anyway.

'How could you let it happen, Nick? You know his triggers, you know how fast it can get serious if he has a major exposure.' Her tone changed again, turning wooden and cold. 'You weren't even there, were you?'

'Look, wouldn't you rather hear how he is now than how it happened in the first place?'

She gave a shocked moan. 'How he is now? You mean—?'

'He's fine,' he cut in quickly, not really wanting to punish her to that extent. 'He had a good night, and he's hungry. He accidentally breathed in some fine ash from someone's campfire. He was stirring it up with a stick and it was still warm and just flew up into his face.'

She made another sound.

'Miranda was brilliant, and so were the medical centre staff.' He didn't tell her how scared he'd been, couldn't control the way his voice softened as he spoke Miranda's name.

'So he's with you? Are you in your cabin? Dr. Carlisle's always good, Nick, you sound as if it's something miraculous. Josh adores her. I wouldn't have let him go up there if she hadn't been going. Can I speak to him?'

'He's still at the medical centre. It's a small hospital, really, they have good equipment on hand. Brand-new, after the cyclone.'

'And you're there with him, right?' she asked, an ominous note building again in her voice as she readied herself for raising her righteous anger by several notches. 'Nick, even though Dr Carlisle is brilliant, she can't give him the same attention as a parent.'

'She would. Always.'

'Always?'

'She would.'

'For heaven's sake, I cannot believe this.' She stopped suddenly, and sighed. 'OK. OK. Just tell me you're with him, that's all!'

Nick felt the familiar stubbornness overtaking his best intentions and didn't answer her challenge. 'When does your flight get in?'

'Early afternoon, but I want to speak to Josh.'

'What time? I can meet you at the airport.'

'I want…to speak…to Josh!' she articulated with cold precision. 'For a man who claims to love his son—' She broke off suddenly, and he thought he heard her sisters' voices in the background, sounding impatient. 'I—I—Just a minute, Nick,' she said in a different tone, then put her hand over the phone so her words to Louise and Bron were muffled. 'OK, OK,' he faintly heard. 'I do see. Yes, I can hear it. I'm not perfect. I can't work miracles on myself. Give me a chance.' The phone clattered and he heard, crisp and clear, 'Sorry, Nick.'

'Don't worry. Josh and I will phone you back,' he told her, and cut the connection because he wasn't confident of his own ability to stay civilised and in control of himself if they kept talking.

Enough with breakfast.

His appetite had gone.

Miranda would probably have come to see Josh at the medical centre by now, and he felt his pulse leap at the thought of seeing her. What time had it been when he'd said goodbye to her at her cabin steps? Three-thirty in the morning? Less than four hours ago, but it felt like a lot longer.

He wanted to hold her in his arms, promise her

the world, protect her and laugh with her and slake his doubts with their two bodies moving together. He wanted to tell her about Anna's phone call, about the repertoire of too-familiar accusations, about the tangled layers of mistrust and miscommunication, and that odd note of bewilderment that had crept into Anna's voice a couple of times. He wanted to hear Miranda promise him something different—faith in each other, shared understanding that happened with words and without them.

But then as he came up the ramp to the medical centre, he saw her through the side window, laughing at something Grace had just said. Miranda tucked a strand of hair behind her ear, and her nose wrinkled when she smiled. To a stranger's eye, from this distance, she could have been little older than seventeen with her lithe build and bobbing ponytail and innocent face, free of make-up.

Grace was laughing, too. The two women looked oddly similar for a moment, although their colouring was not in the least alike. Still, there was something—in the way they laughed, in their sensible approach. They were both the kind of woman that would be a man's best friend, as well as his lover, and who gave too much sometimes.

Nick wanted Miranda with his whole heart and his whole soul at that moment, but the understanding soured as soon as it formed.

With all his baggage, with all his blocks, why on earth would she want to be a part of his life?

CHAPTER TEN

THERE was a buzz of anticipation in the air on Wallaby Island as the camp and medical centre's official re-opening approached.

With memories of last night and Nick uppermost in her mind, Miranda felt it but couldn't fully share in it. Underlying her outward focus, there were questions that wouldn't go away and couldn't be answered, and she could only hope that her preoccupation didn't show.

All of her exchanges with him so far today had been superficial ones, or else very Josh-focused, and Nick's body language could be translated into words of one syllable. *Stay clear. Don't try to get close.* Beyond the body language, she had the definite impression there were things he wasn't saying.

And she'd made a decision. No matter what happened in the future, she knew she couldn't continue as Josh's doctor. Her personal feelings were too deeply involved. Anna—and Nick— would have to find someone else to oversee their son's care.

Tonight, the kids were having a disco as part of the festivities connected with the official opening of the new medical centre and rebuilt camp, and some of tomorrow's invited guests were expected to fly in today.

'Including Stella's dad,' Susie said to Miranda, at the medical centre after lunch. 'She's hoping he won't show up until tomorrow, because she's so desperate to get dressed up for tonight and she thinks he'll say no.'

'Will he?' She'd just finished the paperwork relating to Josh's admission and discharge, and hoped to head out of there soon. To the beach, with a book? Or would she drop in on Nick and Josh?

Susie made a face. 'I'll be stuck in the middle of it all, if he does put his big authoritarian foot down. Stella's roped me in as her stylist!'

'Woo-hoo!'

'Ooh, yes, I'd be looking forward to it, if her dad didn't sound so scary. I'm going to make her look gorgeous, and everyone will see how pretty she can be, including a certain fourteen-year-old surfer type. But listen, the reason I'm here…I've just done a routine physio session with Jack Havens. His chest is sounding very thick, and he feels to me as if he's running a mild temp, says he isn't feeling well. I think you should take a look at him.'

'Where is he now?'

'In the boys' dorm, lying down. He didn't want to go on the rainforest buggy ride.'

'There's a few of them not going, then.'

Miranda had given Nick the go-ahead to take Josh home to their cabin half an hour ago, but she'd also given orders that they weren't to stray too far. She wanted them back for a check-up late that afternoon, and sooner if Josh had any breathing problems at all. If this had been a big city hospital and a normal working week, she would have kept him under medical supervision, but with Nick's cabin so close to the medical centre and having him able to give his full focus to Josh, a continuing hospital stay seemed like overkill.

'Well, it's always a risk with kids like these, isn't it?' Susie was saying. 'They're magnets for every bug going around.'

'I'll take a look at him in the dorm—no sense bringing him here if he's comfortable.' Jack was twelve, and had come to the island without his parents. So far, he seemed to be enjoying his independence, and it would be a pity if his camp experience was spoiled by illness.

'Charles's Lily is still sick,' Susie said, ticking off names on her fingers. 'Robbie Henderson, one of the cerebral palsy kids from Benita's group. Ming Tan sounded a bit snuffly at breakfast.'

Miranda felt a faint prickle of unease, but let it go. 'If my lot all come down with respiratory complaints, we'll deal with it. Beth says they can get extra staff rostered out here if they need to. I've had the Allandale parents and Josh's mum expressing vocal doubts about the calibre of the doctors in a place like this, so far from the city, but from what I've seen so far, I have to say I don't think they have anything to worry about.'

'Oh, absolutely!' Susie said. 'We're very good at keeping the doctors we want and nudging out the ones who don't fit in or pull their weight.'

'Is Jack on his own in the boys' dorm?'

'No, one of the volunteer carers is with him. Jenny someone.'

'Oh, I know Jenny.'

'She's been an asset this week. You don't have to rush over this minute, just some time during the afternoon.'

She left, and a few minutes later Miranda said to Grace, 'I'm out of here for the moment.'

'Pager turned on?'

'Reluctantly, I have to admit.'

Beach or Nick? The question nagged at her again, without an answer.

'Hang on, who's this?' Grace murmured, looking over Miranda's shoulder towards the entrance. 'She's got a suitcase...'

Miranda turned just as the door opened, and there was Anna Devlin. The resort buggy she'd arrived in was turning to go back down the service road. She must have come straight from the airport on the south side of the island and she looked as if she wasn't yet convinced that she was really here. As usual, she took it for granted that her needs and feelings would command Miranda's attention at once.

Which they did, of course…

Because my involvement is way too personal, now.

'Where is he, Miranda?' She seemed jittery, and unused to the bright tropical light, which was making her blink, her sunglasses pushed onto the top of her dark head and forgotten.

'Anna, does Nick know you're here?'

'Not yet. I managed to get on an earlier flight. This place hardly qualifies as a hospital, does it?' Her glance took in the brand-new but compact facilities and Grace's cheerful presence.

'On the basis of size, maybe not,' Miranda said. 'But it's very well equipped.'

'Please, is he through here?' Anna began walking towards the swing door that led to the hospital beds and treatment rooms.

'No, Anna,' Miranda said quickly. 'He's at the cabin, with Nick.'

'You've *discharged* him?' She was horrified. 'But Nick said it was a major attack!' She eyed Grace suspiciously. 'Look, is there somewhere we can talk privately, Dr Carlisle?'

Grace made a covert gesture that said she was happy to stay on hand for moral support, but

Miranda shook her head. She had a few issues, too. She and Anna did need to talk.

'Take the office,' Grace said, but Anna shook her head.

'I need fresh air.'

'Sounds good.'

There was a wooden bench in the shade of a huge fig tree just to the side of the medical centre. Miranda led the way there, not quite knowing what to expect. She had the impression that Anna didn't fully know either. She wasn't quite as hostile or emotional as she could have been. They sat on the bench for several moments in silence. As Josh's doctor, should *she* take the initiative? She didn't know.

Anna closed her eyes and lifted her face to the sun that twinkled through the canopy of the fig tree. She remembered her sunglasses at last, and lowered them into place. 'My sisters staged an intervention yesterday,' she finally began, giving the phrase—deliberately borrowed from drug and alcohol-dependency counselling, Miranda understood—a light, almost self-mocking drawl. 'This week has been so strange and different.'

'It's the first time you've ever been away from Josh,' Miranda guessed aloud.

'The very first. So I tried to put Mum in his place and mother her instead. The nurses looked at me strangely when I asked if they had a fold-down bed so I could stay beside her overnight. They don't. That's for parents with sick kids, or hospice patients, not for a reasonably robust sixty-seven-year-old with a broken leg.'

'Robust?' That wasn't the impression Anna had given about her mother last Sunday.

'After the first shock was over, she did very well. I—I was…really impressed. She did need me for the practical things, but she—' Anna broke off and shook her head. 'She's not frail and, boy, did she serve me one when I tried to treat her that way! She wouldn't let me stay over-night at the hospital. She sent me out shopping. When Lou and Bron arrived—Mum was home by then—she made us go out to dinner!'

'Did you have a good time?'

'We had a blast!'

'Sounds like your mum staged a bit of an inter-vention, too.'

'Oh, it was a total conspiracy! I—I couldn't

believe, when I got home, that I'd forgotten to phone Nick to tell him when I was coming up.' She did the little head shake that Miranda was starting to recognise. It was the movement of someone waking up from a long, unexpected sleep and trying to clear their mind. 'And then, of course, I got his voicemail and got scared.'

'The intervention was about you and Josh…'

'I couldn't see it. I was too close. You tried to tell me, but I couldn't listen. You were—oh, hell, it's so hard to admit it!—right when you said I didn't want Josh to have a good time here because he was having it with Nick. I hated hearing that, but I couldn't forget it. Because it was true. I confessed that to my sisters, geared myself up to betray the darkness of my own heart, and they laughed at me for taking myself so seriously.' She laughed herself. 'They're such witches. Heaven help me, it's good for me! I'm going to make some changes. I have to be honest enough with myself and admit that it might take some time. Show me where the cabin is now, will you? I just want to see him…'

They walked over there together. Knowing where to look, Miranda saw Nick and Josh first, when their brightly coloured holiday clothing was still half-hidden behind a jungle of foliage. They were sitting on the veranda of their cabin, playing a board game and drinking iced juice.

Josh said, 'Your turn…Seven! Hey! That's my hotel!'

'Oh, no!'

'You've landed on it!'

'I know I have! And I have no money!' Nick was convincingly stricken by the prospect of his imminent financial ruin.

'And it costs about a million dollars' rent!' Josh clapped his hands together in glee, while Anna pricked up her ears and stopped in her tracks.

'Oh, wow!' she whispered.

Nick and Josh hadn't seen Anna or Miranda yet. As Miranda went to move forward beyond the concealing screen of foliage, Anna held her back. 'Can we watch? I want to see…I—I don't trust this.'

'Do you want to trust it, Anna?'

'Yes. Oh, of course I do! Maybe it's me I don't trust. He hasn't grown, has he?'

'Not in five days, no.'

'But he looks as if he has some good colour. Not burned. Lightly toasted. He must have been outside a lot.'

'Always with sunscreen.'

'It's great. And Nick looks so relaxed. How long since I've seen him grin like that?' She had tears in her eyes. 'This is hard. Maybe Josh won't even want to see me…'

'Stop. You know that's unreasonable. You're his mother, and he loves you.'

'Oh, hell, I'm scared.'

She stepped out into the open and called her son's name. He looked up, saw her, stood and smiled. 'Mummee-ee!' He came clattering down the veranda steps with his arms held wide, moving faster and more surely than any kid should who'd had such trouble breathing last night.

'Oh, darling, oh, sweetheart…'

They hugged a big, warm exuberant hug.

'Are you having a good time?'

'The best! 'Cept last night. But I'm better today.'

He wriggled out of her arms and Anna let him go. She looked a little helpless for a moment, visibly daunted by her son's increased level of independence in such a short time. But then she mastered the emotional tunnel vision she no longer wanted to feel and managed a smile. 'You look better. You look as if Dad's been taking care of you really well.'

'Come and see our cabin, Mummy.'

'Let me talk to Dad for a bit first, hey? Can you tidy up the game?'

Nick had seen Miranda. Waiting on the veranda, he met her eye and she didn't know what to do. Again, this wasn't professional, it was personal. As Josh's doctor, she could stay discreetly on hand in case Anna had any more questions about last night. As the woman who loved Nick and who didn't know whether it was going to end in happiness or tears, she should probably leave.

His face gave nothing away, gave her no answers. It looked wooden and cautious and she thought he must be far more concerned, right now, with the volcanic shift that had begun in the complex triangular relationship between himself, his ex-wife and Josh.

She would be very much in fourth place, wouldn't she? The fourth kid, the only child latching onto a family of three siblings, playing on the beach. Carefully, she gave a finger wave in his direction and turned to go. He didn't try to stop her.

She remembered her promise to Susie to check on Jack Havens in the boys' dorm, and grabbed to it like a shipwreck survivor grabbing a life-raft. Something concrete to keep her afloat, at least for a while.

She walked in the direction of the dorm, where she found the twelve-year-old listless and achy, with flu-like symptoms that she could only ascribe to some kind of virus—the same one that was making Charles's Lily ill. She pre-scribed fluids and bed-rest, which was all that Jack felt like anyway, and left him in Jenny's care.

'He'll be fine tomorrow, I bet,' Jenny said. 'It's some forty-eight-hour thing. You know what kids are like.'

'Oh, I'm sure.'

There was not much else she was sure of right now.

Miranda had no idea what to do with herself next. The restlessness and tension crippled her and she ended up ten minutes later in her swimsuit on the beach because it was the only place she could bear to go. One of her favourite places in the whole world—sun and sand and ocean and sky, *good* memories, at heart—but she doubted its power to give her any answers today.

Most of the camp kids and parents were still on the rainforest outing, so the beach was quiet. The resort guests tended to stay on the beaches closer to the hotel, unless they were boating or fishing up this way. There were just a couple of boats out towards the horizon.

She went into the water without much appetite for a vigorous swim, just wanting the cool weight of the water around her body, wanting the air and light and freshness as an antidote to everything she was feeling, wanting the physical sensation to remind herself that life did and would go on.

How long would Nick and Anna need to talk? They might be pulling apart their whole marriage and divorce, for all she knew. What would it look like when they put it back together? Did he still have feelings for her? She'd been wondering about that since Tuesday night. If it was only Anna's over-involvement with Josh that had destroyed their relationship, might it not re-kindle?

Oh, of course.

A child was always such a powerful bond.

A night of passion sometimes wasn't.

Miranda had no idea if Nick would even come looking for her after he and Anna had finished saying what they needed to say. She had that first-day-of-the-rest-of-your-life feeling, and there was nothing joyous or new about it at all. Instead, it was a painful limbo, ambiguous and open ended and unsafe.

She'd been there before.

Had been there with Nick himself, ten years ago.

She hadn't wanted it then, and didn't want it now.

Ducking her whole body beneath the water, she wanted to wash this uncertainty away, but it wouldn't leave as easily as that. When she surfaced again and let the salt and wetness stream from her face, she saw him on the beach…

Nick.

Looking for her.

Waiting for her, as she swam and waded back to the shore.

There was an inevitability about it that didn't, all the same, mean his appearance was good news.

He picked up her towel and held it out to her. She took it when they were still at arm's length and the moment wasn't an intimate one, didn't answer any questions, didn't form a connection beyond the brief chain of hand and fabric and hand.

'Hi,' she said, hugging the towel in front of her body as she dried her face and hair. She let her body drip, knowing the sun would dry up the water from her skin very soon.

'I've been looking for you.' His tan had darkened this week, while there were some strands of dark gold bleached into his hair. He had his sunglasses on and she couldn't see his eyes.

'Hope you tried here first.'

'Third, after your cabin and the dining room.'

'In future, try the beach first.' She tried to make it light, but it didn't work, sounded more like a reproach. 'It's one of my favourite places in the world.'

He stepped closer. 'See? I don't know enough about you.'

'No…'

'Because my own damned life—my own problems—always seem to take precedence. Ten years ago. All through this week. And now. I'm so sorry, Miranda.'

Sorry?

Her heart lurched and sank, and her stomach felt tight and ill.

'That sounds like the start of one of those it's-not-you-it's-me speeches, Nick.' The laugh came out shaky. 'Don't, OK? No speeches. And especially not that one. It always rings hollow. Just tell me what happened when you and Anna talked. Are you staying on next week?'

'Yes, down at the resort hotel, I'm moving there today. I checked, and there are rooms available. But, Miranda—'

'So you're moving out of the cabin?'

'It seemed like the only solution. This is all so new, we're both afraid that if I go back to Melbourne tomorrow, the changes we want to make will get lost in old, destructive patterns. This is our chance to cement something fresh, and to do it together. Listen, though…'

'I'm—I'm glad,' she made herself say,

although the words felt like acid burning her mouth. 'For Josh's sake. Divorce is never an ideal option for kids, even when it's the best and only option available. I'm glad Josh will have two parents, united again.'

'Wh-a-at?' He swore under his breath. 'Oh, hell, no! No, Miranda! No, and no, and no! Is that what you think? Is that why you think I'm here? To tell you about Anna and me? That we're starting again? You can't think that the two of us could ever in a million years get back together!'

'No?'

'No!'

'Why? Just pretend I'm not getting any of this and explain. You just said—'

'No, you got it wrong.' He took an impatient pace on the sand. 'I didn't say that at all. And do you want all the reasons?'

'Yes, please…' Her voice shook.

He counted them on his fingers. 'Because it would be much worse for our son than anything he's experienced so far. Because too much damage has been done. Because Anna is focused on fixing her relationship with Josh—and on fixing mine with him, too—not on anything between her and me. Most of all, because it was never right in the first place. Never! I never loved her the way I needed to. I chose her for exactly that reason—because she was safe, while you were so dangerous.'

'Me? Dangerous? I—I'm not dangerous. I'm nice. Boring, even.'

'Boring? You're the most dangerous woman I've ever bloody met!' He touched her at last, fingers light on her neck as if he didn't know how she'd react. Oh, how could he not know? Didn't she have her heart in her eyes, just as he'd said? 'Because I love you. *I love you*. Don't you know how dangerous that is? Feeling it? *Saying* it? It felt so terrifying ten years ago that I ran from it, ran into marriage with totally the wrong woman, but my feelings about you never really changed. I *love* you. If that counts for anything. If it's enough, Miranda. If it's anywhere near enough.'

'Oh, Nick! Enough?'

'Come here. I can't stand not having you in my arms.' He reached out for her and she went, as inevitably as the sun rising over the sea in the mornings.

'*Enough?*' She was laughing, shaking, happy and overwhelmed and still not quite believing what he'd said. His touch began to calm her, began to shift the universe onto the right axis, and then he kissed her hair.

'You can't possibly have got it so wrong...' he whispered.

'Oh, I did. I could. Believe me, I could. But if you love me...'

'If I love you? *If?* Miranda, I love you. I...love...you! And this time around I'm enough of an adult—enough *me*, instead of being my father—not to be scared.'

'Then that's way more than enough, it's everything!'

'Get it right.' He cupped her face, lifting her chin. 'Look at me. Kiss me, and promise me you'll never get it wrong again.' His mouth brushed hers, clung for a moment then let go so she could speak. 'Promise...'

'Even this morning, Nick, after you'd talked about your father last night, you pulled away as soon as you'd said it.'

'Oh, hell!'

'I knew you would. I understand why you did.

I told myself I wouldn't let you do it, but it takes two, and I wasn't sure…I just wasn't sure.'

'So I'd better kiss you until you are,' he muttered.

They stood on the beach with the afternoon sun hot all around them and he kissed her as thoroughly as she'd ever been kissed in her life. He kissed away that morning's distance, kissed an apology for all the times he'd held back, kissed a hundred promises about talking and connection and passion, kissed a million beautiful, perfect words without speaking one of them out loud, and she kissed the same things back to him until they were both breathless.

Some minutes later, he told her, 'I'm the only one moving down to the resort hotel today. Can we get that clear?'

'Good…'

'Anna and Josh will stay in the cabin. Anna and I are going to start dividing up our time with him in a healthier way, and I know now that her sisters and her mother are on side and that she's ready to listen to them, even if there are times when she can't listen to me. I even suggested she go straight back to Melbourne tomorrow, but that was a little too overwhelming for her to think about, and I'm sure I'll still sometimes have to fight her tendency to cling to Josh too tightly, and to shut me out.'

He was silent for a moment and she waited, knowing there was more.

'This is going to take some time,' he began again, slowly. 'Miranda, are you really sure you want to be around when there are no guarantees? When I'm carrying so much baggage? How could I not pull back this morning when I asked myself that question? I'm demanding so much of you. I know it, and you don't seem to, even now. See, you're actually smiling…'

'There's only one guarantee I need, and you've already given it to me.'

'I'll give it to you again.'

'Please…'

They stood there for so long that a wash of inch-deep water from the incoming tide crept around their feet.

'So,' Miranda said. 'A room in the hotel, huh?'

'You're going to get cheeky about this, aren't you?'

'Yep. Getting pretty keen about the hotel room.'

'Nice and anonymous,' he agreed. 'Full of

honeymoon couples who don't even notice anyone else.'

'I have a feeling I might come and visit you there when I have time off, and that I won't notice anyone else either.'

'I have a feeling I might like that. Have a feeling we might have to keep explaining to people that we're not actually, technically on a honeymoon ourselves. Not this time, anyway…'

'Not yet,' she agreed.

'Almost as good.'

'Just as good.'

'With plenty more to look forward to.'

'Oh, yes. Oh…'

They smiled at each other, and saw the future reflected in each other's eyes, the colour of a tropical blue sky with not a cloud in sight.

MEDICAL™

―――∿――― *Large Print* ―――∿―――

Titles for the next six months…

April

A BABY FOR EVE	Maggie Kingsley
MARRYING THE MILLIONAIRE DOCTOR	Alison Roberts
HIS VERY SPECIAL BRIDE	Joanna Neil
CITY SURGEON, OUTBACK BRIDE	Lucy Clark
A BOSS BEYOND COMPARE	Dianne Drake
THE EMERGENCY DOCTOR'S CHOSEN WIFE	Molly Evans

May

DR DEVEREUX'S PROPOSAL	Margaret McDonagh
CHILDREN'S DOCTOR, MEANT-TO-BE WIFE	Meredith Webber
ITALIAN DOCTOR, SLEIGH-BELL BRIDE	Sarah Morgan
CHRISTMAS AT WILLOWMERE	Abigail Gordon
DR ROMANO'S CHRISTMAS BABY	Amy Andrews
THE DESERT SURGEON'S SECRET SON	Olivia Gates

June

A MUMMY FOR CHRISTMAS	Caroline Anderson
A BRIDE AND CHILD WORTH WAITING FOR	Marion Lennox
ONE MAGICAL CHRISTMAS	Carol Marinelli
THE GP'S MEANT-TO-BE BRIDE	Jennifer Taylor
THE ITALIAN SURGEON'S CHRISTMAS MIRACLE	Alison Roberts
CHILDREN'S DOCTOR, CHRISTMAS BRIDE	Lucy Clark

™MILLS & BOON®
Pure reading pleasure™

0309 LP 2P P1 Medica

MEDICAL™

Large Print

July

THE GREEK DOCTOR'S NEW-YEAR BABY	Kate Hardy
THE HEART SURGEON'S SECRET CHILD	Meredith Webber
THE MIDWIFE'S LITTLE MIRACLE	Fiona McArthur
THE SINGLE DAD'S NEW-YEAR BRIDE	Amy Andrews
THE WIFE HE'S BEEN WAITING FOR	Dianne Drake
POSH DOC CLAIMS HIS BRIDE	Anne Fraser

August

CHILDREN'S DOCTOR, SOCIETY BRIDE	Joanna Neil
THE HEART SURGEON'S BABY SURPRISE	Meredith Webber
A WIFE FOR THE BABY DOCTOR	Josie Metcalfe
THE ROYAL DOCTOR'S BRIDE	Jessica Matthews
OUTBACK DOCTOR, ENGLISH BRIDE	Leah Martyn
SURGEON BOSS, SURPRISE DAD	Janice Lynn

September

THE CHILDREN'S DOCTOR'S SPECIAL PROPOSAL	Kate Hardy
ENGLISH DOCTOR, ITALIAN BRIDE	Carol Marinelli
THE DOCTOR'S BABY BOMBSHELL	Jennifer Taylor
EMERGENCY: SINGLE DAD, MOTHER NEEDED	Laura Iding
THE DOCTOR CLAIMS HIS BRIDE	Fiona Lowe
ASSIGNMENT: BABY	Lynne Marshall

MILLS & BOON®
Pure reading pleasure™

0309 LP 2P P2 Medical